Griffin's Way

S.F. Dietrich

I0632775

DEDICATION

To first responders that work so hard at keeping society safe..

CONTENTS

ACKNOWLEDGMENTS

I'd like to thank my beloved wife for her support and encouragement.

Chapter One

He had prepared for this moment for years without knowing it. He had learned trades instead of college. Mechanics before computers. He had learned to use knives from gangbangers in East Los Angeles. He'd even learned anatomy from a book he had read in the library. The art of negotiating he'd learned from agents for the artists he'd worked for. He had even learned religion from street preachers and televangelists and developed his own brand of religion. He swallowed another tab and felt the euphoria spread through his body.

He had purchased the knives months earlier, in a pawn shop in Memphis. It was part of a set of six blades, all daggers. This one was the longest, at sixteen inches. The shortest was a letter opener. All six had twin snakes wrapped around each other for a handle. The guard was ornate and a fake emerald was embedded between the snakes on the hilt. The tails of the snakes formed a guard, and the heads came together to form the pommel. He'd paid cash for the knives and carefully packed them away for this trip. Last night, he knew it was time. He'd taken this knife from his duffel and laid it on his bed. He stroked the blade carefully, like a lover, muttering to it like it was a living thing. He dressed carefully in an old woolen trench coat and left to scout the hotel.

He'd seen her yesterday, dark hair and a serious overbite. Most people would not have recognized her, but he did. He would have known her anywhere. He watched her go in, then about ten minutes later called the front desk asking if she was there, under the name she used. The clerk was very cooperative, giving him the room number when she said she really shouldn't and offered to take a message. He'd thanked her and said no, then hung up. Tonight was the night. Anytime during the full moon would work, but the first night would be the best. To save her soul, he had to destroy her physical body. He knew she would want it too.

He was wearing an old hoody under the coat. With the hood up, he waited patiently by the parking garage, until a car came out, turned right and sped off into the night. Walking quickly into the garage before the door closed, he walked boldly towards the elevators, hands deep into his pockets, hoody pulled forward. He mumbled under his breath as he walked, just nonsense, but a pattern to it. No one stopped him. No one said a word. The garage was deserted.

Keeping his head down, he punched a button to the elevator. It opened immediately and he rode it to the lobby. The doors opened, and he stepped out, keeping his head down and his hands in his pockets until he got to the main elevators, then a quick punch of a button and a pair of doors slid open. He stepped in, pushed a button for the 30th floor. When the doors opened, there was a sign, helpfully indicating that he should turn right. Instead he went left, and walked the length of the hallway. Then he came back, and walked the other direction, past the room, all the way to the end of the hall. There was no one there, he was all alone. No security, no one to get in his way. The door required a key card, but that wasn't a problem for him. He knew that the deadbolt would be locked, and that he'd need a key for it. He had used a stolen credit card to purchase a cheap lock pick set online and had practiced on a door he'd kept in his barn. The lock was a little different, but after thirty seconds, the deadbolt slid back into the door. The credit card he'd used to buy the picks, he used it to slide around the door jamb and he was in. The room was dark, but he could feel her presence. He did not risk turning on a light, instead he held a hand over a small flashlight to look around. He was in a suite, with a door to the bedroom on his right. He walked slowly to the door, praying she was alone in her bed.

The knob turned under his hand, and he slipped the door open just far enough to get into the room. He could hear her breathing, deep and regular. He was close now, salvation for her was at hand.

The light from the street was just enough to see her shapeless form under the blanket. Dark hair over a pillow, the color of coal in the dim light. The knife seemed to will itself out of his coat pocket. Lightly, he slid his hand over the blanket. When he could feel the swell of her breasts, he positioned the knife between them, and angled it straight up. He prayed for his blade to be straight and true, then put all of his weight onto the quillion, shoving as hard and as fast as he could. It hit the sternum and slid off towards him, before finding a soft spot, and sliding through soft tissue. He heard her gasp and start to move, but as the knife went through he pulled it back and forth. It slashed her spine, and she lost all strength in her limbs. He could still hear her gasping as he pulled the knife out and slid it into her again. He could see the blanket on top was turning color and he touched it in awe, as he watched her life blood leave her. Gently he kissed her forehead, and waited patiently until she stopped breathing. He doubted she'd have been heard outside of the bedroom. He groped along the wall, until he found a light switch, then turned it on. He turned to look at her one last time. His mind turned to shock and horror. Something wasn't right. The hair! It was too dark He peeled the covers back from her face, and then stumbled backwards, leaning against the wall. His stomach revolted, but he kept it under control. This was not who he was expecting. He had saved the wrong one!

Chapter Two

Jim Churchill and Sheridan Johnston were placing a table on Sheridan's back patio. They'd been arranging furniture most of the morning. Jim's back ached and sweat was dripping off his nose. He was dressed casually in jeans and an old t-shirt. A Mariners cap was perched on the back of his head.

"Sheridan, you sure this is right?"

Sheridan was close in age to Jim but was dressed in a matching sweatsuit. He was shorter then Jim and stout.

"Looks good to me. Jane is the one that wants it here."

"Sounds good to me," Jim said as he set his end down.

They walked into the kitchen and Sheridan pulled two bottles of beer from the refrigerator and handed one to Jim.

"A little prefunk," Sheridan said.

Jim accepted it gratefully, popping the top and taking a long pull.

"Jim, did I tell you that Jane wants to set you up with one of her friends?"

"About once a week."

"I mean it. She thinks this woman would be perfect for you."

"They'd all be perfect for me. Then they find out I'm a cop and they're gone."

"You're a writer too. Tell them that."

"What do I tell them when the phone rings at midnight, and I have to go?"

Sheridan shrugged. "Jim you gotta give it a try."

"This party was Jane's idea. She thinks we can get everyone together and have a good time. Then we'll get a deal done on the movie and everyone will be happy. I don't have time to have a girlfriend right now."

"That's what I keep telling her. Anyway, this girl is going to be here soon. Be nice to her, okay?"

"I'm nice to everyone, Sheridan. You know me."

"Yeah, I do. That's why I'm asking."

The doorbell rang. Sheridan looked at his watch, and said, "Come on. No time like the present."

They walked to the front door, and Sheridan opened it. A petite, brown haired woman stood at the door. She was wearing flat heels with a black dress. She was wearing glasses and had an overbite, but when she spoke, Jim noticed the distinct sound of Texas.

"Hello Sheridan."

Sheridan hesitated a moment, then said, "Hello Cassidy. This is TW Griffin. TW, this is Cassidy Upton."

They shook hands. Jim thought her grip was warm and inviting.

"I'm a writer," he said lamely. Her green eyes sparkled with amusement.

"Well good for you. Anything I might have read?"

Sheridan started in on a discourse about the four books that had already been written. Jim felt his face flush.

"Sheridan, can you help with my bags?" For the first time Jim looked past Cassidy and noticed an Uber driver standing at the bottom of the porch with a growing pile of suitcases.

"Let me," Jim said and stepped past her before he realized she had six different suitcases, plus a garment bag and a makeup kit. Jim threw the garment bag over one arm and managed to pick up the two largest suitcases in each hand.

"Where too?"

"Upstairs, first door on the left." Sheridan grabbed the two smaller bags and Cassidy picked up the makeup bag. As they went back through the door, Sheridan called out, "Jane, Cassidy's here!"

"Oh good!"

Jane came out of the back. She was a tall woman, her short blonde hair pulled back. She was Jims publisher and good friend.

"Cassidy! How are you!"

The two woman hugged and greeted each other.

"I see you met Jim," Jane said.

Cassidy looked confused. Jim grunted and went up the stairs. Sheridan followed, whispering "TW" as he passed his wife.

"I mean TW. They look so much alike," Jane said, shooting a look at her husband.

Cassidy followed them upstairs and Jim led them in to the guest bedroom. He set the two suitcases on the floor, and laid the garment bag on the bed. Cassidy set her makeup bag on a small table, and Sheridan set two bags down next to the other two. Jane came up with the last two suitcases.

Sheridan explained, "Cassidy was a neighbor of ours in Amarillo. Jane used to baby sit her when she was little. Now she's all grown up."

"Sheridan. You make me feel like I'm six all over again," Cassidy said.

"TW," Jane said, "you'd better get ready. Things start in an hour."

"Yes ma'am."

Jim started downstairs, with Sheridan following him.

"Jim, it's not what it looks like," said Sheridan.

"OK. Because it looks like Jane is trying to set me up with Cassidy."

"Alright, it is what it looks like. But Jim it's not like that."

"It's ok Sheridan. She has nice eyes."

"Is it the overbite?"

"Sheridan, she seems nice. I'll talk to her at the party, see how it goes."

"OK. Jim, I swear this is the last time."

"You keep saying that." Sheridan looked stricken. "It's fine, they've all been really nice. I just don't know if I'm ready."

"Jim, it's been what, ten years? You are ready."

Sheridan turned and went back into the house, shouting over his shoulder, "See you in an hour." He found Jane in their bedroom, touching up her hair.

"What did he say," she asked.

"She has nice eyes."

"Sheridan…"

"So far he likes her."

"How much did you tell him?"

"Nothing. You almost blew it when you called him 'Jim.'"

"She noticed. She's intrigued, but I didn't tell her anything other than he's a writer."

"After this, stop playing matchmaker. Besides, we're running out of friends."

She aimed her hair spray in his direction.

"Sheridan, you're just about the best orthopedic surgeon around. You can afford new friends."

Sheridan changed the subject. "What about the party? Will it break the ice?"

"I hope so. This producer wants to get Jim's book onto the screen in the worst way. If we play our cards right, Jim can retire from the police department and do whatever he wants."

"Which hopefully means more books for you to publish so I can retire while we're still young."

"Doesn't hurt."

"What if Jim marries this girl?"

"Two words. Power couple."

The party was just getting underway when Jim walked back up the street. He was wearing khaki pants and a blue blazer over a white silk tee shirt. He paused in front as a limo pulled up and spoke with an older couple as they got out of the back.

They walked to the Johnston's front door together. Jane answered the door, wearing a soft pink dress. A petite blonde woman stood behind her. Jim did a double take. If it hadn't been for the eyes he would not have recognized her.

"Paul and Linda, so nice to see you. TW, this is Marianne Wilson." Jim shook her hand, it was soft and warm.

"So nice to see you again." Marianne/Cassidy smiled, "Thanks for coming." She was four inches taller than before too, with her high heels. Her black dress ran to mid thigh.

"Everyone else is in the back," Jane ushered them through to the courtyard.

Jim and Marianne found themselves standing together near the bar. Jim handed her a glass from the bartender. "I'm not sure what's in this, but Sheridan usually gets the good stuff."

"Thank you."

"That was pretty good. Was that some kind of dental prosthetic?"

Marianne nodded as she took a sip. "You know who I am, right?"

Jim nodded, "You sing. I went to your concert last summer."

"What did you think?"

"You're pretty good. You don't miss a note."

"Thank you. So, Jane and I lived two houses apart. She's about ten years older than me, and babysat me for a few years. She and Sheridan got married when he was still in Med School. He interned in Seattle, and when he was done, he stayed."

"Some of that I know. They went back to Amarillo every couple years."

"Right. I still have a ranch there, and they stay there, whether I'm there or not. They've been inviting me to come up forever, but my schedule kept getting in the way."

Jim sipped at his drink.

"I came to town for this," she gestured around the yard with her free hand, " I spent a couple nights in a hotel before I told Jane I was here. She told me to come right away, and that she wanted me to meet you."

"You haven't been here before?"

"Well, once, about ten years ago. Where you live was an empty lot then."

"About six years ago, I sold my first book. I bought the lot, and had the house built. Sheridan told me the lot was for sale and said if I didn't buy it he would."

"She called you Jim before, but now it's TW?"

"I'm TW Griffin." She nodded.

"Why Jim?"

He looked around. "That's my real name."

Marianne raised an eyebrow.

"It's complicated," Jim said, "but it makes life a little easier."

"Um hm. So you hide behind your real name. Genius."

"Also cheaper then getting a false overbite."

Marianne smiled and laughed. Something inside Jims chest stirred.

"So, this party is supposed to get our people talking. You're making a movie." It was more comment than question.

"I don't really want too. I've never written a screenplay, and I really don't know how to start. But Hal, my agent, is insistent. He think's it's a good idea."

She nodded. "I'm a singer, not an actress. But Hank does represent some actors. Are they going to do it?"

He shrugged. "Sheridan agreed to put this together. Jane is my publisher so they thought a party might break the ice. When I asked Jane about it she suggested bringing you in."

"I'm flattered," Marianne said, "I'd be happy to write something. Maybe put together a soundtrack."

As they talked they leaned in close to each other and lowered their tone. They moved about the floor, occasionally stopping to talk to some of the other guests. Jim talked to a producer, who introduced him to a screenwriter. Marianne stayed and chatted briefly, then went to get herself another drink.

She was standing next to the bar, holding her drink and watching Jim, when an unfamiliar voice said, "Didn't I see you on the cover of Vogue?"

"Yes you did. Two years ago."

He was a short and pudgy man who was leering at her.

"I knew it. You're a model, right?"

Marianne was conscious of someone behind her, but said, "I'm sorry, I don't speak English."

"Come on, baby, you don't have to be like that..."

Jim's voice from behind her said, "There's a phone call for you ma'am."

Marianne turned gratefully, and said, "Oh please, show me where."

The pudgy man started to follow but Jim put a hand on his chest. "Alec, she doesn't need your help."

He took a step back. Jim stared at him a moment, without blinking. Alec turned and walked back to the bar.

They walked into the house and she said, "That guy gives me the creeps."

"Me too. That's Alec MacNair. He has a bit of a reputation. Did he tell you he could get you a part?"

"He was working up to it. He had some cheesy line about me being a model."

"Yeah, he thinks he's being suave. He really didn't know who you were?."

"You didn't have to step in. I had it under control," Marianne said.

"I could see that. Look over there." Jim pointed with his chin across the room where a photographer was shooting pictures. "If you'd done anything to him, the fallout would have been on you."

"Damn photographers. Who's he with?"

10

"Free lance. Jane hired him but you bet your ass he'd make copies of everything. You feel like getting out of here?"

"Yes! so long as I don't have to hear another pickup line."

He took Marianne by the hand and led her through the living room and out the front door. She looked around before stepping outside and then they walked quickly to his garage. He took her through the side yard, and across his lawn to the boathouse. Jim pressed a series of buttons on the door, and it opened under his hand. Inside, suspended from a pair of large canvas straps, was a Sundancer 370.

"What's it doing up there," Marianne asked.

"I keep it on the hoist to keep it clean." He hit a switch on the wall, and a motor hummed to life as the hoist lowered the boat into the water with a small splash. It took just a moment to disconnect the shore power and water, and open the outer door to the lake. Then Jim helped Marianne aboard after suggesting that she take off her high heels. He climbed into the cockpit and started the twin mercury motors. As the dashboard came to life he pointed out the various instruments and explained them. She was fascinated by the Chartplotter, when he explained how it was tied into the radar so they could see other vessels around them.

Jim backed out of the slip, then when he was clear of the boathouse, pulled back on one throttle, and forward on the other. The boat spun to the right, and when it was lined up with the middle of the lake, Jim pushed both of the throttles forward. The powerful motors pushed the boat up and out of the water, quickly getting on plane.

"There's beer in the fridge," Jim gestured towards the bar area just behind the cockpit, "or if you'd rather, something stronger in the galley."

Marianne was smiling, and shook her head. "Later," she said. The wind made it hard to hear. She took a seat next to Jim in the cockpit, their thighs touching. He glanced at her from time to time, as they paralleled the floating bridge across Lake Washington. He liked watching her, green eyes alight, hair blowing back in the wind. Just as dusk was beginning to set, they entered Union Bay. Jim pulled the throttle back, slowing the boat to 7 knots.

"That was fun. I'll take that drink now," she said.

Jim gave her the wheel, and told her to hold it steady along the right half of the canal as they passed Husky stadium. He went below, and came back a few moments later with two glasses holding an amber liquid and ice cubes.

"I'm impressed. Where did you get ice cubes?"

"When I'm not using it, I keep it plugged in to shore power. Let's the refrigerator run, so I keep a couple trays in there."

She took a sip. "Hope it's ok,"he said, "It's Jamesons, and I didn't have anything to mix it.".

"Perfect." She let him take back the wheel, brushing against him as he slid past her.

"Why do the Johnston's call you Jim," she asked.

Jim paused a moment. "My real name is Jim Churchill." She took a sip, then made a go ahead gesture. "I'm a cop. For the last eighteen years. Now I'm a lieutenant out of Homicide. I met Sheridan about eight years ago."

As they passed through the Montlake cut, Jim pointed to the bridge, and told her about talking a man out of jumping off.

"How high is that?"

"About fifty feet. It's survivable, but it'd hurt."

She nodded. "I called him Roger," Jim said. "The way he wore his hair, reminded me of Roger Daltry. The first sergeant that got on scene was named Roger. He thought I did it to screw with him."

Marianne laughed. "Tell me, how did you meet Sheridan and Jane."

"Sheridan saved my leg. Maybe my life. Jane I met later."

Marianne raised her eyebrow. "Tell me about it."

"Not much to tell. I got shot by a guy that was trying to steal a car. Sheridan is probably the best orthopedic surgeon around. He happened to be at Harborview hospital when I was brought to the emergency room. The bullet shattered my tibia, and he put it back together again. When I was rehabbing it, Sheridan would check on me every so often. He suggested putting my thoughts down on paper, so I did."

"That's how you got into writing?"

"Yep. He looked at what I'd written, and took it to show Jane. She's on the board of my publisher, and after some rewrites, she got the first book printed."

"And the rest is history," she suggested.

"I can't complain. That first book paid for the house and my first boat. I wanted a bigger boat, so I wrote another book. Now I'm four books in, and doing ok."

"Is there a scar?"

Jim pulled his left pants leg up. Just below the knee was a small round scar, with a narrower scar running down about six inches. She reached down and touched it with a finger, tracing the scar down his shin. Jim seemed to have trouble breathing, and could feel his face getting warm.

She looked up at his face and started to say something but stopped. Jim looked at Marianne for a moment and they both forgot where they were. Then the alarm on the dash started blaring.

Jim looked up, and spun the wheel to the left, pulling the left throttle back as he did so. The boat spun back, then he straightened it out, just missing the wall on his right.

Marianne sat back in her seat, then on impulse leaned over and kissed his cheek. Jim felt a little thrill surge through him.

"I'm starving," she said, "I didn't eat a thing. Do you have anything to eat on this barge?"

"Not exactly. But, how do you like seafood?"

Marianne said, "Ok," but sounded dubious.

Jim reached into his coat and pulled out his "personal" cell phone, the one he used as TW Griffin. He pulled a number out of his contacts, and when the connection was made asked, "How's things on the dock?" He listened for a moment, then ordered two salmon samplers and a bottle of Pinot Noir. He said, "About ten minutes," before ending the call. Jim turned to Marianne, and asked, "Can you wait ten minutes?"

"Maybe I can nibble on my shoes or something."

After a slow drive of about eight minutes, Jim slid the big boat up to the dock. He tossed out the fenders and using the bow thrusters brought the boat alongside. Marianne watched as he tossed the bow line to a young man wearing a waiters apron, then raced aft, grabbed the stern line and jumped onto the dock to tie off the stern, as the waiter finished up front.

"Ivar's Salmon house," Jim said to Marianne. When he looked up at her, she was wearing a pair of oversized sun glasses in spite of the gathering dusk. The waiter waved to someone at the top of the ramp, and a waitress brought two boxes and a bottle down to the dock. Jim signed a paper, and handed the boxes up to Marianne. "Hit and run today guys. Thanks much," he said as he undid the bow line, then the stern line and jumped back on board. He eased the boat away from the dock, and headed towards the center of Lake Union.

"I thought you were going to ask me to go inside," she said.

"I would have, but you seemed reluctant."

"It's a pain in the ass sometimes. If I go out to eat, the next thing you know is, I'm surrounded by cameras."

"I wondered. When I go to a book signing, I wear a fake beard. You should try it."

Marianne punched him in the arm.

They ate dinner in the middle of the lake at a table Jim set up just aft of the cockpit and sitting next to each other on the sofa. Marianne loved the food, but only ate about half. They each had a glass of wine. Jim offered another, and she accepted.

They talked some more and he asked her about her singing. She told him about singing in front of thousands of people. "To be honest, I sometimes get a little stage fright. But once I'm out there it just melts away."

"I've met so many great people and fine artists. People I would not have known about if it wasn't for my work. My backup singer is the sweetest person and she has such a great voice." She went on about some of the people. "I've had this one roadie, He knew my dad when I was little, but we lost touch with him. Years later, he turns up at one of my concerts. Turns out he'd been working for Springsteen, and he'd had a couple concerts with groups like the 'Stones. I personally think he did a little too much acid, but he knows his shit and works his ass off at a show. And I've never seen him high."

Jim nodded. "I know some guys like that."

Marianne nodded. "I sent him through rehab before he started with us. Told him if he messed up, he was done. He was great."

"Was?"

"One day he just left the bus and didn't come back. We had to leave without him. He had a cell phone but he never answered it and never called back."

"What happened to him?"

"No idea. I got ahold of a cousin of his, and they were going to file a missing persons report. They never said anything so I assume he's still out there somewhere."

Marianne had another glass of wine, then shivered. Jim took off his jacket and slid it around her shoulders. "It's getting dark. We better get back."

He started the boat, and headed back through Portage bay, into the Ship Canal. She snuggled into his shoulder, and he wrapped an arm around her. He stroked her hair before settling down to guide the boat through the canal.

"What are you thinking," Jim said to the top of her head. She murmured something into his shoulder, and Jim said, "What?" Before he realized she was asleep. They came out into Union Bay, and Jim started heading back across Lake Washington. He cut the throttle, about halfway across and pondered his predicament for a moment. Carefully, Jim lifted

14

Marianne, and gently eased her onto the sofa at the rear of the cockpit. He went down into the cabin and came back a moment later with a blanket to cover her. Then he eased the throttle forward and drove back to his boathouse at a considerably slower pace.

Back at their house, Jane and Sheridan were cleaning up after the party.

"I noticed Marianne and Jim never came back," said Sheridan.

"They were smart. I did not like the way that Alec talked about her. Or looked at me for that matter."

"He did not like it when you told Alec you thought Marianne had a boyfriend."

"I know! Who the hell is he? I don't know him."

"He's a producer is all I know. Alec MacNair. I'll look him up."

Chapter Three

Marianne opened her eyes and saw the ceiling of the boathouse overhead. She thought about the night before, then opened her eyes wide as she realized she didn't remember anything from the ride back. Gently she lifted the blanket, and saw she was still dressed. She dropped the blanket and closed her eyes. Breathing deeply, she opened them again. She realized she could smell coffee, and something else. She could hear a voice, talking low from a little way away. She pivoted on the sofa and slowly stood. She peeked down the stairs and saw Jim talking on his phone.

"Good morning," he mouthed , "coffee?

She nodded and he handed her a cup as she stepped off the ladder.

"What the hell happened last night," she said when he had hung up his phone.

"You fell asleep on the ride back. I put you to bed. By the way, Jane wants you to call. I texted her last night, but she called me asking about you this morning."

"Where did you sleep?"

He pointed at the couch. "There." She saw a lifejacket at one end, and a blanket. His shoes were sitting on the floor.

"Why out here? There's a perfectly good bunk right there," she said, pointing towards the bow.

He ignored the question. "Cornbread," he asked as he opened the oven door, and pulled out a pan.

"You made this? Here?"

"I had some eggs left in the fridge, and a mix in the cupboard." He cut out a wedge and set it on the table with a jar of honey and a plate of butter.

As she ate, she asked if he had a shower on the boat.

"No, but we can go up to the house."

Marianne finished, "That was delicious. Where's my purse? I need to call Jane."

Jim reached up to the cockpit, and picked up her purse. "This is heavy." He set it on the table.

Marianne reached in and pulled out a .380 pistol.

"Sig Sauer," Jim said, "6 rounds. Newer model, rainbow finish."

She set it on the table. "Weighs about a pound. I can put all six rounds in the bullseye, touching each other, at twenty five yards."

"Nice."

She pulled out her cell phone, and dialed a number from memory. Jim realized she was talking to Jane, and went up to the cockpit. She came up a moment later, and realized he had pulled into the boathouse and left the door open. A cool breeze was coming in off the lake. Jim had his sport coat in hand, and draped it over Mariannes shoulders. She adjusted it, then picked her shoes up from the deck.

Jim helped her off the boat, then used the switches on the wall to hoist the boat out of the water and close the door. Marianne noticed the shore power was hooked up.

"You were up early."

"No matter what, I cannot seem to sleep past five. But I hooked up last night when we came in."

He took her hand, and they walked up to the house. To unlock the door, Jim held his thumb up to a screen. The lock clicked, and they went in.

"This is actually the basement," he said. The west wall was all glass, and faced the lake.

He showed her the rooms in the basement. On the left was a large room. On one side was a weight set and a treadmill. On the right, was a small room, he called his "safe room." Inside was a large safe, and two smaller ones, bolted to the floor. The largest one looked like he could live inside it.

When he got to the middle door, he said, "You might like this." He opened the door. Inside was an electric piano and guitar. "I call this my music room. When I get writers block, sometimes I come here and play guitar."

17

"Nice guitar," she said.

He picked it up, and strummed a couple chords, then launched into the first line of "Blackbird." Then he handed it to her. "Try it out."

She plucked a couple strings, made an adjustment, then launched into the opening stanza of 'Layla.' Then she set it back on the stand. "Nice."

They headed upstairs. On the middle floor was a large living/dining room and kitchen. Off to one side was a formal dining area. Marianne thought it had probably never been used. The kitchen was trimmed out in cherry wood and stainless steel appliances. There was a Keurig machine on the counter.

The top floor had the master bedroom at one end. There were four guest rooms. The master and two of the guest rooms had their own bathrooms. When he showed her the walk in closets, she noticed several suits, some with Armani labels on one side, along with various pants and shirts. Everything was in order and seemed to be at some level of organization. There was a large linen closet in the hall.

Marianne checked out the shower. "Is that a stereo in the shower?"

"Yep, you can get all the hits."

Marianne laughed as she turned it on. One of her songs started playing over the speakers. She looked at Jim, who's face was turning red.

"It's got a Bluetooth feature."

"I see you're the one buying my records. Thank you," she said.

Jim reached past her and turned off the stereo. Not knowing what to do, Jim suggested they head back to the Johnston's.

"Do we have to? I'm enjoying myself."

Jim smiled.

Marianne said, "You know, Jane fancies herself a bit of a matchmaker."

"I'm aware of that."

"The first thing she said to me when I told her I was in town was that she wanted me to meet her neighbor."

"Well the old guy across the street is still married, so that doesn't leave many alternatives."

She smiled. "I was wondering what you thought about that."

"I'm hoping she knows what she's doing."

Marianne sat on the edge of the bed, and leaned back. Her black dress seemed to merge with the black quilt on his bed. Jim stood awkwardly in front of her.

"Where do you do your writing?"

Jim said, "Down the hall I have an office." His voice was thick. "Sometimes downstairs if I'm so inspired. Most of the time, I'll take a couple weeks off and run up to my cabin or out to the coast. No phone, no distractions, just me and a laptop."

"You've done well for yourself. What do you like the most about writing?"

"That I'm limited only by my imagination. I can write whatever I want, and that's the only thing slowing me down."

Marianne shook her head, shaking her hair out of her face. "One more question."

"Shoot," said Jim.

"Are you gonna kiss me, or what?"

Jim felt a lump forming in his throat, but he stepped forward and bent to give her a quick kiss. Marianne wrapped her arms around his neck and pulled him down on top of her and kissed him hard.

Chapter Four

Jim woke up to Marianne shaking him. For a moment he forgot where he was. Then he heard his jacket ringing. He got out of bed and scooped it up. Jim fumbled for his work phone from the inner pocket and answered. Marianne could hear his side of the conversation, which was limited to, "OK," "Yes," and taking notes at the table under his window. Finally he said, "I'm about an hour and a half out," and then he hung up.

Marianne looked at him, a question on her face.

"I've been on call since noon. I completely forgot. There was a homicide downtown last night. I've got to go in."

Marianne asked, "When will you get back?"

"Not sure. It could be late. Stay as long as you want."

"The rest of my life?"

He smiled, "Sure," Jim said as she smiled back at him.

Jim went into the bathroom, showered and shaved. He was back inside of two minutes, then disappeared into the closet. Marianne expected to see him in a suit, but when he came out Jim was wearing a pair of pants with cargo pockets and a golf shirt, over a pair of sneakers. A Glock was clipped on his right hip. A spare magazine and handcuffs on his left. A small flashlight was next to the magazine.

"Is that a nine millimeter??

"No, a forty." The .40 caliber Glock had been a standard issue for years.

" How well can you shoot that," Marianne asked.

"I'm a fucking surgeon with it," said Jim.

Marianne smiled. "I bet I could do better," she said.

Jim smiled, "You're on." He picked up her phone, and dialed a number. A moment later his personal cell started buzzing. He ended the call, and typed something on her phone, then did the same with his. Smiling again, he said, "You have my number now. If you need anything, call me."

She realized a change had come over him. It was subtle, but she could see him becoming more businesslike.

"It's 1:30 now. I could have dinner for you if I know when you'll be back."

He looked surprised. She was sitting up in the bed, the sheet covering her body. He stepped in and kissed her again. "I'll call you. I mean it. Stay as long as you like." Than he added, "I'm not sure what's here, but you can check the kitchen."

He grabbed a windbreaker and tugged it on, kissed her again, reached around behind her and gave her butt a squeeze. Marianne squealed and jumped, then kissed him again. Then he was gone.

Marianne heard the garage door roll up, and a car start up and drive off. Looking around, she spotted her dress laying on the floor. "Crap, I can't wear that." She got up and stretched. Naked, she padded across the floor to the bathroom, and stepped into the shower. When she was done, she toweled off and looked around. She found her underwear, and reluctantly slipped them on. She didn't have a bra, but she found a robe. He did not have a hair dryer. There was a dresser in the corner. In the second drawer she opened, she found a t shirt and slid it on. Looking at herself in the mirror, she realized that on her it was more like a short skirt than a shirt. Jim was much bigger than she was, so she knew she wouldn't find any thing else that fit. Reluctantly she called Jane.

"Hi honey. You ok?"

"You have no idea. But I have a little problem. Could you bring me some clothes?"

"Oh honey, what did you do?"

"Bring me some clothes and I'll tell you everything."

As soon as Jim left the gates of his neighborhood, he hit the siren and lights in his unmarked Explorer. He drove like the professional he is, but a part of his mind was still in the house, with Marianne. He thought about kissing her, before he could force himself to focus completely on the drive. It was a short trip across the 520 bridge, mid afternoon on a Sunday.

He got off the freeway and cut across mid town to the Olympus hotel. There were two police cars in the driveway, and two unmarked units. The CSI van was already there, but no sign of the medical examiner.

Jim left his Explorer in the driveway, and headed to the lobby carrying a notebook under his arm. He took his badge off his belt and showed it to the concierge, who directed him to the elevators. He rode up to the 30th floor, and turned right off the elevator. Room 3003 was halfway down the corridor. A patrol sergeant and officer were standing in the hall outside. Two detectives were inside the room, standing back from an inner door. Both were wearing gloves and paper boots on their shoes. The officer handed him a pair of the booties, which Jim slipped on over his sneakers. He pulled a pair of latex gloves from his pocket and put them on.

"Lloyd, what do we have?" Lloyd Murray was a tall, big man, with a sharp mind. He was the most seasoned detective in the unit. His partner, Ross Nolan was short and trim, with dark skin.

"Lieutenant, Abigail Dunbar is in town on business from Knoxville Tennessee. She came in with a group, but she was the only woman, so she got a room to herself. It's a tech company, making GPS systems under contract to Sea Ray. They're here to meet with Microsoft folks about software programs."

Ross chimed in. "She's also a major in the Air Force reserve." He looked back through his notes. "They checked in Saturday night. She didn't come down for breakfast. She's generally the first one up, but no one thought anything about it. Her assistant knocked on her door about 10, but she didn't answer. By 11, they asked the front desk to check on her. The assistant went in with the manager, and they found her stabbed to death in her bed."

"She have any family here?"

"No, her husband is in Knoxville, he manages a bank. The assistant told her husband and he's coming out. We haven't verified it yet, but it sounds like he never left town."

"Alibi her coworkers. CSI finding anything?"

"A ton of shit. This guy left evidence everywhere," said Lloyd.

"Great, maybe I'll be home for dinner."

"Don't count on it. But take a look at this." Lloyd showed him the door. There were scratches on the bolt. "It's a little early, but looks like the door was picked."

"Professionally?"

"Probably not. Anyone can learn how to pick a lock by typing 'how do I pick a lock' into a search engine. Come in and look at this. Just don't touch anything."

Jim ducked under the tape and followed Lloyd to the bedroom. The CSI crew was taking samples from blood smears on the wall and door.

"I think he panicked for some reason and fled. She was targeted, but this guy panicked."

"Who would target an executive that makes GPS?"

"A competitor?"

"Maybe. I dunno. This feels like something else."

Jim looked at the body for a moment. Something seemed familiar about her, but he couldn't place it.

"He picks the lock. Sneaks into the bedroom, then drives a knife through her heart." He looked at the wall behind him, and reached an arm out.

"He stabs her, then reaches for the light switch." He was being careful not to touch the wall. The blood behind him was smeared.

"I bet his fingerprints are in the blood. Look, you can see them on the switch."

One of the CSI's spoke up. "Be careful el tee. We pulled fibers off the wall, and you're right, those are fingerprints. But right here, the blood is smeared. I think he backed into the wall after the blood was there."

Jim and Ross were quiet, watching him work. "Something surprised him."

"What? Knock on the door?"

"Something else maybe. He turns the light on and sees something he didn't expect."

"Someone else in the room." Jim turned to Ross. "Check with the manager, see if someone else was sleeping here. Also, pull tapes for the night of the murder."

"Done. Also, we asked for the tape from the night before."

They moved to the hallway, to give the techs room to work.

"OK, good idea. He might have scouted the place. Maybe he picked her up. He could be a guest in the hotel."

"That's going to be a lot of work. Can we get some help on this?"

"How about the usual? I'll get the guys from intelligence to watch the tapes too. Has anyone canvassed the rooms on this floor?"

"The rooms on either side are empty," said Ross. "We've covered the entire floor, and spoken to a half dozen people. We are working on getting the names of everyone that was here the night of the murder, and one floor up, and one floor down."

"OK. Have someone check the stairwells."

"They're alarmed. We can get a key from the manager, and we'll have someone walk it all the way down."

The homicide sergeant came down the hallway. Sergeant Mike Worthy was several years younger, with the lanky, wiry build of a rock climber.

"I got your message, Jim. Stopped at Starbucks." Mike was carrying a cardboard drink carrier, with four large coffees, and a white paper bag. Lloyd and Ross each took a coffee. Jim took a bill from his wallet, and handed it to Mike, then took a coffee, and the paper bag.

"Sorry to eat in front of you guys, but I am starving."

"Skipped breakfast, boss?" Lloyd was smiling.

"Slept in this morning."

Lloyd looked at Ross and raised an eyebrow.

Lloyd spoke to the patrol sergeant, who got on the radio and asked for four more officers. They arrived together about ten minutes later, the manager right behind them. Lloyd instructed them on what to look for and two went to the stairwell nearest the room. The other two went to the other end. It was just moments later, when the sergeants cell phone rang. The sergeant answered, and spoke for a few minutes, then approached Jim.

"Four floors down, my officers found a coat with blood on it."

Jim leaned in the door to the room. "Ray, grab your kit."

Jim and Ray, with Lloyd following, went down the stairs. Halfway between the twenty sixth and twenty seventh floor, they found the two officers standing next to an old, wool coat. There were clearly blood stains on the front, and blood on the railing. Ray went to work, taking photographs of the coat. Then he took samples of the blood he could see on the railing. The coat itself, he carefully placed inside a white paper bag.

To the officers, Jim said, "Nice work. Check all the way down." The officers reluctantly turned and started down. Jim, Ray, Lloyd and Ross all headed back up to the 30th floor, carefully scanning for anything else and not seeing it.

When they got back to the room, the medical examiner was inside, examining the body. "No sign of sexual assault," she said, "the body appears to be posed, but she definitely was killed here."

Lloyd asked, "can you estimate the time of death?"

"Based on liver temp., sometime around midnight last night, give or take an hour."

"Welcome to Seattle," said Jim.

He was sitting on a bench across the street from the Olympus. He'd seen the first officers arrive and then a sergeant around five minutes later. That was followed by a battered Crown Victoria and two plainclothes cops had got out. Both were big men, the passenger was black. He saw them scan the area and he bent his head to take a bite of his ice cream cone. 'Nothing going on here, just a guy eating ice cream,' he thought.

It was more than an hour later when an Explorer pulled into the turnout. By then he'd taken to laying on the bench. This one was big too, in a different way. He looked around once, his eyes coming to rest on him for a moment, before moving on. Once the man went inside, he got off the bench and shuffled away, trying to look like he fit in. He'd been there too long anyway.

It was eight in the evening when they took the body out, and pronounced that they had gotten all they were going to get. The manager gave them three discs, one of the lobby for Saturday night to Sunday morning, one of the thirtieth floor, and one of the bar. Lloyd asked if they had a camera for the street view, and was told yes.

"We need that as well." They went to the lobby. Jim told Lloyd and Ross he'd see them in the morning at the office, and went to his car. When he pulled his phone out, he saw it was dead. Jim started the car, and plugged in the car charger.

When they got into their car, Lloyd said to Ross, "Did you notice the lieutenant said he slept in?"

"What's that all about?"

"Dunno," said Lloyd. Must have been a good vacation."

Jane got off the phone from Marianne, and went up to her room. The bed had not been slept in and a garment bag lay unzipped on top of the covers. She zipped up the garment bag, and picked up the largest suitcase. She opened it and decided it wasn't right. Jane grabbed another suitcase, and opened it, liking it better. She opened a third suitcase, and transferred some underwear and socks to the second case. Then she grabbed the garment bag and the second largest suitcase and went down to her garage, dumping the bags into the back of the golf cart they kept there. Jane went back upstairs and grabbed a makeup case before returning to the golf cart. She went back inside, and found Sheridan in his office, looking at what seemed to be a set of x-rays.

"I'm running over to Jims house dear."

Sheridan grunted.

"We'll be running away together to a tropical island."

"That's nice dear."

She sighed, and went out to the garage. It wasn't that they didn't love each other. When Sheridan got wrapped up in his work he had a tendency to exclude anything else. Come to think of it, it was something he and Jim had in common.

Twenty minutes after the telephone call from Marianne, Jane pulled into Jims driveway. Looking around, she decided no one was watching. Jane slung the garment bag over one arm, and grabbed the suitcase and makeup bag and went to the front door. As she was trying to figure out how to ring the doorbell, Marianne opened the door.

"Oh good! Thanks for getting here so quick." Marianne grabbed the suitcase and makeup and they headed upstairs.

"That t shirt looks good with a belt," said Jane.

Marianne agreed and said, "I still want some real clothes on."

"What happened last night? We saw the two of you leave on his boat, then Jim sent Sheridan a text saying you fell asleep and he didn't want to disturb you."

"He is so sweet," said Marianne, and told her about the boat and take out from Ivars and then falling asleep and waking up in the boathouse.

Jane took it all in, then asked, "You didn't call me until almost two. You're leaving out the good stuff." She pointed at the unmade bed. Her question was unspoken.

Marianne sighed. "I couldn't help myself. You know I wasn't sure he was going to, and then it just happened."

"Well, I'm glad. He's a nice guy. A little quirky sometimes, but nice."

"What do you mean?"

"His work. He's like Sheridan when he's working. When I left, Sheridan was looking at a patient file. I suggested that Jim and I were running away together, and he just said, 'that's nice.' Jim is like that. He's a lot of fun, and smart and there's an edge to him, but when he's focused on work it's like there is nothing else."

Marianne had slid into a pair of torn jeans that covered her butt nicely. She'd taken the belt off the t shirt, but left the shirt on. She was using Jims desk as a vanity, and had a hand mirror propped up to put on her makeup.

"What are you going to do," asked Jane.

Instead of answering, Marianne said, "Why didn't you tell me he is a cop?"

"He would not want us too. We have these functions and when he's there, he wants to be introduced as TW Griffin, the author. Not Jim Churchill, the fuzz."

"Has he said why?"

"Look around the neighborhood. How many cops could afford a house in here? It's easier when they think of him as the author."

"Kind of my opposite."

"He told me once that there's only one guy from work that he would trust to know the truth. Even he doesn't know everything. I think he told his boss that he lives with TW to provide security."

Marianne finished off her lips, and said, "how do I look."

"Like a million bucks, as usual."

"What should I do?"

"About what?"

"About Jim. Should I stay here? Go back to your place? I want to make him a nice dinner and play house with him, but I don't want to be pushy either."

"Sheridan is not going to notice I'm gone for the next several hours. Why don't you and I go shopping."

"Excellent idea. I'm thinking about getting a crock pot."

Chapter Five

It only took a few minutes for Jims phone to charge up enough to turn on. When it did, he saw he had several messages from his agent, and two from Marianne. The first one asked what he would like for supper. The second was asking to text her when he was on his way home. "But stop first," it said, "I'd hate for you to get a ticket." It ended with a smiley face. He replied he was on his way. His agent's messages were variations of "Call me now." Jim decided he could wait. It was never as urgent as Hal made it seem.

Lloyd and Ross went back to the office. Ross burned a copy of the DVD from the hotel, then sent the original to the video unit with a request for a dozen copies. Then he plugged the DVD into a computer, and he and Lloyd watched the video start to roll.

"What time did she check in?"

"Just after one in the afternoon," replied Ross.

"OK. Take it to 12:30 and lets watch it from there."

They let the video scroll forward, until a few minutes before one, Abigail Dunham strolled into the lobby with three men. She was wearing a conservative business suit, as were all three of the men. It being a Saturday, none of the men wore ties. Abigail, however, wore a scarf around her neck. She stood erect. Lloyd, who had been a marine, and Ross, who had been in the army, recognized the military posture. They'd already talked to the three men with her. None had mentioned her being in charge, but here it was plain, the men were deferring to her.

Abigail and the men walked to the counter to check in. There was no sound, but the two detectives were trying to read body language. Abigail handed the cards to each of the men, then took the last room for herself.

"She's making sure the others are billeted before she takes a room," said Lloyd. "You see anything that looks like resentment on their part?"

"Nothing at all."

They watched it again, then a third time.

"Hold it a sec..". Then Lloyd spoke again, "Run it again, but focus on this guy." He pointed to a man in the lower left corner.

They watched as he walked into the frame. A short, pudgy man. He was openly leering at Abigail's backside. At one point he grabbed at his crotch, and made a comment to someone out of the picture. Then he walked out of frame.

"What's in that direction."

Lloyd closed his eyes and thought for a minute. "The bar. Bring it up."

The bar spooled out before them. They saw the new guy walk into the bar and order a drink.

"Middle of the afternoon, and he's already drinking?"

"Ross, I think we need to talk to him. And the sales guys, all three of them."

Ross called the hotel and spoke to the manager. He spooled up the video on his own computer, and saw the guy they were talking about.

"I'm not sure if he's a guest or not. I can print out the picture and ask the manager."

"Call him. Get him in there to look at it."

"It's the middle of the night. He's asleep."

"There was a homicide in your hotel. He'll come in."

Lloyd called Jim on his cell phone. It rang four times, then Jim answered. He sounded awake and alert. Lloyd thought he heard a woman's voice in the background, and chose to ignore it. He explained that he wanted to send a bulletin out with the picture, requesting an identity on the man in the video.

"OK, they call you. No probable cause for arrest. ID and call you, right?"

"Exactly."

"Then go for it. Send it to the Attorney General for statewide distribution. First thing in the morning, go back to the Olympus and show that picture around. When does the husband get in?"

In the background he heard, "she was married? I bet.." then she was cut off by Lloyd saying, "8AM."

"OK, Ross takes the picture around. I want you to meet the plane. In fact, send the photo to all the airlines. Maybe someone will remember him."

"Yes sir. Sir, do you have company."

"Say good night Lloyd."

"Good night, Lloyd."

Lloyd hung up, and looked at Ross.

"El Tee has a girlfriend."

"Are you sure? When was the last time he was on a date?"

Lloyd thought for a minute, then said, "He hasn't been serious with anyone for, what, ten years?"

"Even if he was, he wouldn't tell us about it."

"True," Lloyd said, "Do you think he remembers what to do?"

"You heard her on the phone. What do you think?"

Jim pulled into his driveway close to nine. He jockeyed the Explorer around and backed into the open bay. Jim slid out of the car and hit the down button for his garage door as he walked into the house. Across the short hall was his laundry room. The door was open and he could see his clothes from the night before hanging up, clean and pressed. He walked into the kitchen area, and saw Marianne in his living room. She was sitting cross legged on the floor, a pair of headphones over her ears. She would pause, and write on a pad of paper. He watched her for a moment, her forehead wrinkled in concentration and decided he liked what he saw.

"Hi Jim," came from behind him. He turned, and saw Jane and Sheridan in the kitchen. "She's been like that for a couple hours. I think she's inspired."

"I'll leave her alone then, " he said as he took a glass of wine from Sheridan. "What's going on?"

"As a medical professional it's been left to me to discuss the birds and bees with you."

"Thanks Sheridan, but I prefer to learn about that in the gutter, like all my friends did."

"Sheridan, stop that," Jane said, "Jim, we've been holding dinner for you."

"My God, thank you. I had something earlier, I think. Oh yeah. It was a Starbucks sandwich."

"You poor thing."

"I hope you've been enjoying my wine. Is that the good stuff?"

"Nothing but the best for your friends, Jim."

Jim took a plate, and carried it into the dining area. Jane and Sheridan sat on either side with their own plate. Jane brought another for Marianne. Jim walked over and touched Marianne on the shoulder. She looked up, and her face lit up.

"Jim," she said as she stood up, and hugged him. "I've been writing for hours. I didn't hear you come in."

They returned to the table, and Jim asked Marianne about her writing.

"Just from whatever is going on at the moment. I'm working on one now about how you can be surprised by what life brings you." She looked suddenly shy.

"What's the process like? Do you write the lyrics to match the melody or the other way around?"

"This one, I wrote the music earlier, now I'm trying to write the words. I'm playing the music on the stereo to help."

"She's been at it since they got back," said Sheridan.

"I'm surprised you noticed we were gone," said Jane.

"I notice everything my dear."

Marianne tried changing the subject. "Jim, tell us about your case."

"A woman from out of town was stabbed to death in her hotel room. There's a ton of evidence, we should be able to wrap this up soon."

Marianne made a give me more gesture, so Jim went on. "She's from Knoxville Tennessee. Have you ever been there?"

"The last time was about three years ago I think. I was on tour and we did a concert there. Didn't stop though, we had to be in Nashville the next night, so after the concert we drove straight through."

"Do you get back to Nashville much?"

"About once a year for the CMA's. I have a house there, and staff. I love it, but I don't get back enough."

They talked some more about Mariannes' career, and what it's like to play in front of crowds of people. Sheridan and Jane were looking at each other knowingly.

"Do you work tomorrow, Jim?"

"Afraid so. I'm going in a little early, there's some things I need to do. I probably ought to get to bed."

They said their good nights, and Jim showed them to the door. Marianne said she'd be along in a bit, that she was going to clean up. As they shook hands goodnight, Sheridan leaned in and whispered to Jim, "Don't rush her off. She wants to be here tonight." Jim nodded, and then said goodnight to them both and closed the door.

Jim walked into the dining room. The table had been cleared off, and the plates were in the dishwasher. He went around the floor, to turn off the lights. Before heading upstairs he saw the doors to his balcony were open. He went through the door and saw Marianne standing against the railing, staring out over the lake. He walked up behind her and slid his arms around her waist. She leaned back against him and he kissed her neck.

"I was saving a glass of wine for you," she said. He accepted the glass from her and clinked it against hers.

"I'm glad you stayed."

"I asked Jane if she thought it would be rude to stay here another night. She told me not to worry about it." She chuckled at the memory of Jane telling her that Sheridan knew where the key to the wine cellar was.

"I'll be honest. Usually after a day like today I grab a frozen meal and stick it in the microwave. It's been a long time since I've had a home cooked meal waiting for me."

"Jane told me. She say's she tried to set you up a few times, but nothing ever came of it."

"Between my work and my writing, I just didn't think I could."

"So is anything different?"

Jim leaned his butt against the railing and sipped his wine.

"Not sure. What I do know is that since I left this afternoon, I couldn't wait to get home again."

Marianne stepped up to him. Her head was at chest level and Jim had to lower his head to kiss her. It was long and drawn out and when they broke he could feel his face was flushed.

"Do you mind if I spend another night here," Marianne asked.

Jim shook his head, "I was hoping you would."

Marianne pushed away from Jim.

"Give me five minutes, then come upstairs," she said.

Jim smiled, "Starting now."

Marianne gave Jim a quick peck on his lips, then ran into the house and disappeared upstairs. Jim followed her inside, then closed and locked the door. He set his glass on the counter, then looked at his watch. Barely three minutes had gone by.

"Fuck it," he said, then walked upstairs.

He opened the door to the bedroom, and saw Marianne, kneeling on the bed, wearing a pink, high neck baby doll nightgown. Instantly, he felt his throat thicken. She did not say anything as he approached. He stopped in front of her and she put her hands on his chest. He kissed her, and Marianne slid his windbreaker off his shoulders.

Afterwards, they lay still. It took some time for breathing to come back to normal. Both were naked, and their skin was shiny. Marianne was snuggled into Jims side, smiling happily, her head on his shoulder.

A cell phone started ringing. Marianne sat up, startled. "Tell me you're not being called out?"

"Probably not, just a minute." Jim fumbled through his pants until he found the right phone, then answered it. Marianne lay back on a pillow, her eyes closed until she heard Jim say, "When does the husband get in?"

Marianne sat up again, an instant wave of sadness as she said, ""she was married? I bet he's devastated."

Jim hung up from Lloyd, an exasperated look on his face.

"What," she asked.

"One of my detectives heard you on the phone. By the time I get to work, it's going to be all over the building that I have a girlfriend." He was sitting on the edge of the bed. "What do I tell them?"

"Tell them that Cassidy Upton is one classy broad." He laughed, and kissed her. Then he kissed her again, longer, and then he pulled the blanket over their heads as he laid her back down on the bed.

Chapter Six

He picked up the knife. Not as nice as the first one, but it would do. Identical but two inches shorter. He laid it on the floor, and knelt, naked. He lifted his hands in prayer and mumbled incoherently. Then he got dressed and laid down to sleep.

Jim arrived at the office at seven, an hour late. Lloyd looked up and checked his watch. Lloyd was unshaven and his hair was unkempt. Shocked at the time, he grabbed an electric razor and a mirror from his bottom drawer, and shaved at his desk, then straightened his tie before heading out the door on his way to the airport. Ross was pulling in another detective, Jason King, to help with his interviews. They were on their way back to the Olympus.

Lloyd stopped at Jims office door on his way out. "I've got to run, but we went to the autopsy this morning."

"Anything we didn't expect," asked Jim.

"No. No sign of sexual assault and no DNA transfer. But his fingerprints are in the blood on the wall."

Jim sat at his desk and logged into his computer. While he waited for it to boot up, he looked at his notes from the day before. Finally, his computer blinked and asked for his password. He typed it in, and while the computer finished the process, Jim made some more notes. His computer blinked at him again, and he clicked on his time sheet. Jim entered the overtime from the day before for his detectives and his sergeant, and then himself, then closed the sheet, and clicked on his email. Since he had been on vacation his email had piled up. He checked up the list, opening each one before moving to the next. There were a half dozen emails from the weekend but finally he opened the bulletin that Lloyd had sent out the night before.

"Aw shit." Jim looked out to the bullpen. Only Fred Henderson was still at his desk. Jim sat back down and pulled out his cell. He called Lloyd, but got no answer. He called Ross, but his phone was off. Lloyd, he figured, was in the airport or on the road. Ross was probably in an interview.

Jim pulled his desk phone over. He used the computer to search for the number to the Olympus and found it. It was answered on the second ring.

"Is Alec MacNair registered there?"

There was a moments hesitation and then, "Yes sir."

"I'm on my way. Have someone from security meet me in the lobby."

He strolled out of his office, "Fred, you're with me." Fred Henderson picked up his coat and hustled to keep up with Jim.

"What's up," Fred asked, as he covered his girth with a cheap sport coat.

"The case that Lloyd and Ross are working on. We're going to talk to the guy in the bulletin."

Jim tossed the keys to Fred, and told him to drive. As they backed out of the parking lot, Jim called Ross again. Still no answer, so he left a voice mail, then he called Jason. He answered on the third ring.

"Jason, Jim Churchill here. Where's Ross?"

"He's talking to Abigail's assistant. I guess his employment status is up in the air, and he's spilling some stuff."

"I'm on my way to the Olympus. As soon as you're done there, call me."

Fighting traffic, it took twenty minutes to get to the Olympus. Fred parked in the turnaround, and buzzed the valet. Both of them headed in to the lobby. A florid faced man in a cheap blue sport coat introduced himself as "Ted, from security."

"Ted, we need to know which room Alec MacNair is in."

"Sir, I understand, but we have to respect our guests privacy."

"You understand this is a homicide investigation?"

"It doesn't mean that…"

Jim did not have time for this. "Get me the fucking room number, before I bring in a bunch of financial auditors to tear your fucking books apart. They'll have this hotel out of business so long it will be bought out by motel 6."

Ted paled. "You don't have to do that sir. He's in room 3503. I have the card key."

"You're kidding." Then, "OK, come with us." To Fred he said, "That's directly over the victims room by five floors."

As they got on the elevator Jims phone buzzed. He answered it, and said, "Meet us by the elevators, thirty fifth floor."

It took a few minutes, but finally the doors opened. Jason and Ross were standing on the landing.

"The guy in your bulletin is Alec MacNair. He's a producer with a bit of a shady reputation. At least that's what the tabloids say."

"Will he talk to us?"

"He might. This is your case, so you take the lead."

A little after one in the afternoon, Lloyd walked into the bullpen. Jason and Ross were talking excitedly with some of the other detectives from the squad. Lieutenant Churchills door was closed, and he was typing on his computer.

"What's going on?"

"Lloyd, you wouldn't answer your phone. Hey, who is this?"

Lloyd turned to the man with him. He was a large and powerfully built man, who looked incredibly sad. "Alan Dunbar, my partner Ross Nolan." He introduced them around. "He's going to wait in the lunch room. Hector is going to sit with him." Hector Alvarez was a civilian employee who worked as a victims advocate. Hector took Mr. Dunbar by the arm, and walked him to a lunch room, leaving Lloyd with the other detectives.

Ross started, "You should have been there." LLloyd made a go ahead gesture. "The lieutenant calls us and has us meet him on the thirty fifth floor. He says he knows who the guy in the bulletin is, and I should talk to him. We go to the room, and just as I'm getting ready to knock, Jim tells me to hold on. Then he listens at the door for a minute, and gets this weird look on his face. He tells the security guy to open it."

"What happened?"

"The guy tries to open it, but one of those privacy locks is on the other side. So Jim fucking kicks the door open! The lock goes flying off, and Jim goes through the door gun first! Jason and I are right behind him, and I'm all 'what the fuck.' I come around the corner, and I see this guy standing there, his dick in his hand and a fifteen year old on the floor in front of him. She's crying, and her clothes are half tore off. And Jim says to the guy, wait, what did he say, Jason?"

"'Move and I'll decorate the wall with what's left of your brains."

"Yeah. But it was the way he said it. Total deadpan. I'm telling you, I think if we hadn't been there he might have killed the guy."

"Shit." Lloyd looked at the lieutenants office a touch of admiration crossing his face. "What's he doing now?"

"Writing a love letter to the chief, explaining why he pointed his gun at that motherfucker."

Just then, the lieutenant's door opened. He had his jacket off. "Hello Lloyd. We brought your guy in."

"I was just hearing about it."

"Don't believe everything you hear."

Jim told a much more sanitized version, and finished with, "Special Assault wants him when you're done with him. Fred is standing guard outside the door until SAU secures a warrant."

Lloyd picked up his file. "You want to sit in?"

Jim said, "No. I think that might be counterproductive. I'll watch from the other room if you need me."

"OK. What do we have on him?"

Ross chimed in. "Alec MacNair, lives in Los Angeles, and has an apartment in New York. Nothing in Knoxville. Two years ago he was picked up for soliciting a prostitute, when he propositioned an undercover LAPD detective. The charges were later dropped, after he went through some kind of rehab. Rumors circulate that he uses his position as a producer of movies to exploit young actresses, which he auditions personally. Let's see. Married, no children. It appears his wife lives in the apartment in New York."

"Good." Lloyd, Ross and Jim headed to interrogation. Ross and Jim went into the observation room. Lloyd waited a moment, then walked in. Alec MacNair was handcuffed behind his back, sitting at the table.

"You're still handcuffed? Here, let me take those off." Alec leaned forward and Lloyd took the handcuffs off. "Are you thirsty? I brought you a water."

"Can I get a coke?"

36

"Sure, in a minute. Right now, Water is all I got. How you doing?"

"I'm ok. Who are you?"

"I'm Lloyd Murray. I'm a detective. Can I ask you a few questions?"

"I had no idea she was fifteen. She told me she was twenty two."

"Oh, thanks, I'll pass that on. I'm not here about that."

"What do you mean?"

Lloyd had said in the bulletin that Alec was a "Person of interest." Ross had read Alec his Miranda rights at the scene, but since he wasn't actually a suspect in the homicide, Lloyd didn't need to advise him. Yet.

"What brings you into town, Alec?"

"Do you know who TW Griffin is?" Lloyd nodded. "He's in negotiations with my firm to turn his first book into a movie. We've been talking to his people all week."

"How's that going?"

"I'm not really sure. TW Griffin is kind of a straight shooter. If this gets out, I might lose the contract."

"How come?"

"He walked out of talks with a director when he found out he was sleeping with his kids nanny."

"That must be tough finding someone that's not sleeping around in Hollywood."

"Man, I'm telling ya. The trim you can get in that town."

Behind the glass, Jim thought, "yeah, you lost the contract all right."

Lloyd asked, "Where did you stay?"

"The Olympus. All week. Best hotel in this town."

"Tell me about Saturday."

"His publisher had a reception at her place in Hunts Point. Beautiful place, right on the water."

"What time was the party?"

"I got there about four. It was in full swing."

"Who was there?"

"Dr. And Mrs. Johnston. It's their place." He named a couple other executives. "Oh, Marianne Wilson. TW of course."

"Marianne Wilson the singer?" Alec nodded. "And they can verify you were there?"

"Well Jane, sure. She kept coming on to me the entire party, but I was spending most of my time with Ms Wilson."

"OK, what time did you leave?"

"About ten."

"Alone?"

"Well, Marianne was going to come with me, but I ditched her at the last minute."

Jim laughed. Ross looked oddly at him.

"OK. So you left at ten. What time did you get back to the hotel?"

"About eleven. I went to the bar and had a drink, then I went straight to bed."

"By yourself?"

"Yeah, by myself."

"OK. How do you know Abigail Dunbar?"

"Who?"

"Abigail Dunbar."

"I have no idea who that is."

"Alec, I have video of you talking to her in the bar."

"I still don't know who that is."

Lloyd took a picture from his file. It was her Air Force publicity photo.

Alec studied it for a minute. "Oh, yeah. I was in the bar, and she came on to me."

In the corner was a television and DVD player. Lloyd took a disc from his file and plugged it into the machine. "Watch this Alec."

The machine spooled up the video. Jim watched as the soundless video played. Abigail was sitting at the bar. Alec, looking drunk off his ass, waddled over to her, and tried to talk to her. At first she tried to brush him off, Jim could almost hear the words, "I'm not interested." Alec seemed to get angry, and grabbed Abigail by the arm. She threw her drink in his face, then made some kind of small compact move, and Alec fell to the floor. She said something to the bartender, and walked out. Alec lay on the floor for a moment, then slowly got to his knees. When he could stand up, he shook his head, and stumbled out of the room. No one seemed interested in helping him.

"That doesn't look like she was coming on to you, Alec."

"OK, maybe I remembered it differently. Fuck, my balls still hurt after seeing that."

Jim was smiling inside. At least Abigail was a fighter.

"Did that make you angry, Alec?" Lloyd spoke quietly.

"Hell yeah. I just wanted to show her a good time, and she knocked me on my ass."

"Did you follow her, Alec?"

"Hell no. I'm not that stupid. That bitch could have killed me."

"What time did you get to your room, Alec?

"About ten minutes after this video. And I went straight to bed."

"By yourself?"

"Yeah. I struck out."

"That's no good Alec." Lloyd pulled another picture from his file. This one of Abigail in bed, with the knife in her chest.

"Oh fuck," Alec said. His face turned ashen. He retched suddenly, then turned and vomited onto the floor.

"I'm sorry," he said in a tiny voice.

"Alec, who were you with?"

"I don't know her name."

"Tell me about her."

"She's a hooker. I paid her fifty bucks to come back to my room for an hour. She got there about midnight. She left a little after one. Am I in trouble?"

"Where can we find her, Alec?"

" I called an escort service on my room phone. They sent her. They said she was clean, but the bitch stole my Rolex."

"Alec, it wasn't your night, was it?"

"How much trouble am I in?"

"Alec, you were caught trying to force a thirteen year old to have sex with you. Nobody gives a shit about the hooker. And I'm the murder police. If you didn't kill Abigail Dunbar then I don't give a shit about you either. The sex cops are on their way to pick you up."

Lloyd put Alec back into handcuffs, and came out of the room. "He didn't do it."

"No he didn't," Jim agreed, "but he's still going down for rape of a child. It would have been way too easy if he had killed Abigail."

Lloyd's phone rang. He spoke for a few moments, then hung up. "Good news and bad news."

"Good news first, please."

"We got DNA from the handle of the knife, on a male, white, mostly European descent. Probably between forty and seventy."

"OK."

"Bad news. There is nothing in AAFIs for prints, and DNA is not on file."

"Well, there's nothing like a good mystery. Looks like we'll have to do this the old fashioned way. Did you talk to the husband?"

"He's in the lunchroom. He wants a room at the Olympus. Said he'd feel closer to his wife."

"What's your take on him?"

"He said they've both been faithful. They met at a joint training conference. He was a Lt. Col in the army, she was a captain. Dated about a year, got married, transferred to the reserves. He's a Colonel now in the Tennessee National Guard. She's still Air Force reserve. They've been in Knoxville about five years. He's been deployed once, her twice. Said he's never looked at another woman since he met her, and she's the same way about him."

"What about work?"

Ross chimed in. "Her assistant said she's the best boss he's ever had. Same with the other two guys. They respected her. However, the assistant said she was constantly fending off advances from her boss."

"You saw the video. It can't have gone well for him."

"No. She filed an EEO complaint against him. Knoxville PD has him listed as a missing person, and he missed a court date for DUI about a week ago. They're investigating an embezzlement case with him, and they think he fled the country with whatever money he had on hand."

"OK. Get as much information on the boss, and see if we can track his movements. Lloyd, I want to meet Mr. Dunbar."

Lloyd walked with Jim to the lunch room. Alan Dunbar and Hector were talking quietly as Lloyd and Jim walked into the room.

"Mr. Dunbar, I'm so sorry for your loss."

"Thank you."

"Is there anything I can do for you?"

"When you find him, let me have a few minutes alone with him."

"If only it were that easy," Jim said. "We will do our best to keep you appraised of any developments. I have to ask, is there anyone you can think of that had it in for Abigail?"

Alan thought for a minute, "The only guy that I know that hated her enough to do this was that asshole boss of hers. Arnie Thompson."

Jim raised an eyebrow.

"She'd come home from work and tell me stories. Arnie would get drunk at lunch, then come in and try to put his hands all over Abigail. He told her once that if she didn't give it up to him her ass would be out on the street. She said she smiled at him, then grabbed his tie and tightened it until he couldn't breath and told him if he didn't back off she'd quit and tell the board of directors what he was up to."

"Knoxville is looking at him for embezzlement. What's that about?"

"I don't know much about that, except that he's on 'leave without pay' pending the criminal investigation, and that he skipped town. Frankly, I don't think he got much. He really wasn't all that smart."

40

Lloyd and Jim left the room. "Make sure he gets into his room ok. I don't want him free lancing."

Lloyd nodded. Two SAU detectives were walking Alec out of the room. They were taking him to their offices at the other end of the floor. As they passed, Alec looked at Jim and said, "You kicked my fucking door in, you asshole. That's an illegal search! I'll have your badge!" Jim said nothing, simply stared deadpan at Alec, his eyes gone black. Alec's eyes got wide. Lloyd and Ross both thought Alec was starting to pass out. The detectives hustled Alec down the hall.

"I really wish he was the guy," said Lloyd.

"A guy as sexually frustrated as he is, wouldn't have just killed her," said Jim.

Lloyd and Ross nodded.

"I think we've done all we can today," Jim went on, "You guys need to get some rest. We'll get together first thing in the morning. Someone may have to go to Knoxville."

Lloyd said, "Can we send Jason? I think the answer is going to be here. Not Knoxville. There's still something about this that doesn't feel right."

Jim nodded. "OK. You're the lead. Make sure he gets copies of everything you have before he goes. I want everything we have on her boss."

"You got it, lieutenant."

Chapter Seven

It took Jim over an hour to get home in rush hour traffic. He parked the explorer in the garage, and went into the house. Marianne was not in the kitchen or living room. He felt a twinge of disappointment. It was still early, so he went upstairs, and changed into sweats. Then he went back downstairs to the basement. As he was walking to the basement gym, he passed his "music room." He stopped when he thought he heard something, and went back. Listening at the door, he could hear Marianne singing, "Storms Never Last." He cracked the door. Marianne had her back to the door, and was wearing headphones. He could see his electric guitar was strapped across her chest. She had on a black t shirt and tight blue jeans. Jim watched her as she sang. He waited until she finished, then applauded.

Marianne turned around, and smiled. "Hey baby, you're home!" She unslung the guitar, and got it hung up on the chord from the headphones. It took her a moment to get untangled before she could give Jim a kiss.

"Honey you sound fantastic."

"I'm supposed to sing it on television."

"When is that?"

"About six weeks. Can you come?"

"I don't see why not." Jim promised to check the schedule the next day.

"Did you solve your case?"

"Well no, but we did make an arrest." They moved up to the living room as he told her about Alec MacNair.

"I can't say I'm surprised. He's a creep. Who caught him?"

They were sitting on the couch. "There was a bunch of us there."

"Was it you?"

"It was a team effort."

"It was you wasn't it?" Her eyes were bright.

"Well, I was there."

"I knew it. He's such a creep. He kept coming on to me at the party."

"He said he ditched you."

Marianne laughed, her eyes bright. Then she told him, "He's got a reputation."

"Really?"

"What I've heard is that he has 'auditions' and brings in young girls, then forces them to accommodate him."

"With this kind of thing, other victims start showing up. Those poor guys in sex crimes are going to have to sort through the ones that are really victims, and weed out the ones that are looking for a payday."

"People do that," Marianne asked.

"It happens. But they got him pretty cold on what happened today. These guys tend to have a pattern of behavior so the detectives will be able to figure out who's telling the truth based on how much they deviate from the pattern."

"Well you done good, Lone Ranger. We should celebrate. Let's go to a club," she said.

"You ever hear of 'The Lime,'" Jim asked.

"No, what's it like?"

"Never been. But I hear on the radio that it's '80's night."

Jason arrived in Knoxville early the next morning. He rented a car on the departments credit card, and drove from Alcoa to Knoxville, using his GPS to locate the Knoxville Police station on Howard Baker drive. He found a small diner along the way and had a plate of over cooked scrambled eggs and hot coffee. He drove the rest of the way with a queasy stomach, but arrived right at nine am, local time.

Jason parked in the visitor lot. Inside the lobby was a reception area. He approached the counter and told a sergeant why he was there. The guy sounded bored, but he dialed a number and said, "Guy here says he's a Seattle Police detective to see someone about the Thompson case."

Jason asked, "How many cops you guys have?"

"Around 350, give or take."

A door opened behind the sergeant, and a burly black detective came in. "Bert Kling. Who are you?"

Jason showed his ID and badge, and said, "Jason King. Seattle Police Homicide. I was told you'd be expecting me."

"Well shit, no one told me. Message must not have been passed on. Come on in." A door buzzed and opened in the wall, and Jason followed Bert inside. They took the stairs to the second floor. "Always take the stairs when you can. It's healthier," said Kling. Jason didn't respond. He was focused on his breathing and keeping his breakfast down.

In the office Bert pulled a file, and said, "The best place to read this is probably right here. We have an empty desk in the corner," and gestured towards a desk in the back of the room, shoved up against a wall. Bert set the file on the desk.

Jason thanked him and sat down. Bert went back to his desk. Jason opened the file and began reading. After about an hour and a half, Jason stood and stretched. He'd shed his coat and loosened his tie.

"Hey Bert, you have any coffee?"

"Yeah, I'll show you."

They went into a break room, and Bert took down two cups. "They're mostly clean," he said, as he poured Jason a cup.

"Ah yes, just like home." Jason took a sip. The pot had been sitting a while and Jason did not think it would do his stomach any good. "Can I ask a couple questions?"

"Sure."

"I didn't see much criminal history. Anything that didn't go in the file?"

"No, it's all there. A DUI, and a pop for illegal gambling."

"It says he's got two cars, and both are accounted for. How did he get out of town."

"We don't know. We figure he got a ride from someone he knew."

"Any idea who?"

"None yet. TBI is working on it."

"Who is TBI," Jason asked.

"Tennessee Bureau of Investigation. They help out on fugitives."

"Can I make a suggestion?"

"Sure."

"Check his ex wife's house. It looks like there's an attachment there."

"We talked to her. She said she hasn't seen him."

44

"Did you search the house?"

"We asked. She wouldn't consent."

Jason paused for a moment. "He's in there. She picked him up and drove him there."

"We can't get in there without a warrant. No way will she consent, even if he's not there."

"Set up surveillance. I bet within a couple days you'll have enough to go in."

"I've been waiting for you to tell me what your interest is in him."

"It's waning, but one of his employees was murdered in our city."

"Which one?"

"Abigail Dunbar."

"She took his position when he left."

"So she was a boss?"

"She'd have got it sooner or later. In the meantime she had all the responsibility and none of the pay. She had some testimony that would help against Thompson, but nothing critical to the case. What made you pick him?"

"We have evidence that Thompson was infatuated with Dunbar. He's a person of interest in   her stabbing."

"Mind if I take a look?"

Jason didn't mind. They walked back to the desk, and Jason took a file out of his briefcase. He opened it, and showed the pictures to Kling. Kling looked at her Air Force photo. "I remember her. She was smart." He flipped to the picture of her in her bed, a knife through the blankets and stuck in her chest. He looked hard at the picture, then flipped through others until he found a series of pictures of just the dagger. He looked at the handle, the twin snakes intertwined and the fake emerald.

"Hang on a second."

Kling walked to a clipboard containing a stack of bulletins and carried it back to Jason's desk. He was leafing through the stack, when he found the one he was looking for.

"Check this out." Jason looked at the bulletin. It detailed property taken in a burglary about six months ago. Among the property taken was a set of six knives. Jason realized he was looking at a photo of the murder weapon.

"Where is this from?"

"Memphis," Bert pointed out the phone number on the bulletin.

"Can I get a copy of this?"

"You bet."

While Bert was making the copy, Jason pulled out his phone and started calling.

Chapter Eight

Jim opened his eyes and stared at the ceiling for a moment. His gaze wandered around his bedroom until they encountered the form sleeping next to him. Marianne was on her stomach, naked, amid the twisted bedsheets. A look at his watch showed it was 5AM. Marianne was going to have a hell of a headache he thought. His own head was pounding. He stood, and stumbled to the bathroom, where he washed his face in cold water, and sucked some down from the faucet along with two aspirin. That helped, but brushing his teeth made it worse. He grabbed a robe and went down the stairs to make coffee.

He made two cups, and went back upstairs. He set one of the coffees on the nightstand next to Marianne, along with two aspirin. From underneath the mass of blond hair, he heard, "You're staring at my ass, aren't you?"

"I take the fifth."

"My God, you're like a teenager."

"Not today. I don't think this hangover would allow it."

"Well that's too bad. I hope last night was worth the sacrifice you make today."

"It will carry me through. I should be ready to go by tonight though."

"Oh geezus."

Jim smiled and went into the shower. In five minutes he was clean and shaved. Marianne had rolled over and was sipping at her coffee, as Jim stepped into a pair of pants to one of his suits.

"Anything on your case?"

Jim checked his phone. "Jason made it to Knoxville."

"Knoxville! Tennessee?"

"That's the one. Why?"

"Seems like a long way to go. What's the connection?"

"Kind of tenuous. Her boss was caught embezzling from their company. He's checking it out."

She sat up. The sheets slid down to her waist.

"If you think it's going to be a dead end why did you send him?"

His voice seemed thick, and it was hard to get air out. When he spoke, it felt like it was coming from far away. "We have to check it out. Sometimes the effort pays off."

Marianne picked up her coffee, and took the aspirin. "Jim, you're going to be late."

Jim nodded. He kissed her roughly and with great reluctance stepped back. She smiled sweetly and said, "straight to work now."

Lloyd was on the phone when Jim walked into the office, almost an hour later, wearing sunglasses. Ross was watching a video on the computer. "What do you have, Lloyd?"

Lloyd covered the receiver with his hand. "Just a theory I'm trying out."

"What's that?"

"What if Abigail wasn't the target? What if it was a case of mistaken identity?"

"We're coming up empty everywhere else. Give it a look."

"Hey, lieutenant. How's your love life?"

"Not for public consumption, Lloyd."

Jim went into his office. Lloyd came in behind him.

"I'm serious lieutenant. I heard her on the phone the other day."

"Lloyd, she's bright, intelligent and talented. I'm definitely punching above my weight here,"

"The important thing is, you're out there fighting."

"Back to work Lloyd."

"Yes sir." Lloyd stepped out of the room.

A tall, thin, angular man stepped in.

"Good morning, Captain." Captain William Daniels was in charge of the violent crimes section.

"It's good to be back, Jim. One can only stand sun and surf for so long."

"You've seen the files on this case?" Daniels nodded. "Jason King is in Nashville, talking to detectives there. Arnie Thompson is a long shot, but I figured better safe than sorry."

"Yeah, good. Good. Anything else?"

Lloyd is following up on some leads. He's working a theory that might have some merit."

"OK. I'm still getting caught up on emails, but the chief wants a briefing."

"Good luck with that."

Captain Daniels chuckled, and said, "You're coming with me."

"Aw no."

"It's not a request. I was enjoying the beaches of Hawaii until yesterday. I'm still getting caught up and you know the case. The chief is having a cow about the budget, so maybe play down the Nashville thing."

"Or play it up. I'm hoping to hear from Jason soon."

"Your call. But be careful. Meeting's at two."

Marianne stood and stretched before answering her phone.

"Marianne? Jane."

"Good morning. I was working." Paper cluttered the floor where she'd been writing, using Jims guitar and piano to play out the medley's.

"Excellent. You could use another hit."

"Thanks a lot!"

Jane switched the subject. "Have you seen the paper?"

"Jim doesn't get a paper."

"I'll be right over."

Marianne closed her phone and went up to the middle floor. She loved the view and had finally been getting into a rhythm.

The door rang, and Jane was standing there, holding a copy of 'The Seattle Times.' She came in, and headed to the kitchen. "I need coffee."

While the machine was spitting out coffee, Jane handed the paper to Marianne. It was folded back to the entertainment section. A picture of Marianne with the caption, "Singer Marianne Wilson was spotted at The Lime in Kirkland last night. Witnesses said she was canoodling with local writer TW Griffin."

"Well shit. I knew this would happen. They didn't get Jim in the picture."

"Lucky him," said Jane.

Marianne pursed her lips.

"Right now, this is local," Jane said, "in a few hours it's going to be nationwide. The Lime will be happy, it'll put them in the spotlight."

"It's a decent place. Maybe I should sign a photo."

"Stop it. You can't go back there, at least not right away. The media will be there for sure."

"Well fine. What do you suggest for lunch?"

"Hectors. They're usually discreet. Why don't you put Cassidy together."

"I can't eat with her overbite. I've got some big sunglasses I'll wear. I've got to tell Jim about this."

Marianne thought for a minute, then sent a text.

Jason was driving west on Interstate 40 approaching Crossville when Jim returned his call.

"I hear you have a lead on our murder weapon."

Jason had his phone on the blue tooth speaker in the rental car. "Yes el tee. It was taken in a burglary in Memphis about six months ago. I'm on my way to talk to the detective and look at the file."

"I have a budget meeting in an hour. Do not answer this phone until you've talked to him."

"Understood. I'm hoping to get to Nashville by six tonight. I should be in Memphis by nine. I'll get a cheap room someplace and call you in the morning, after I talk to the detectives."

Jim rang off. Five minutes later, Jason's phone rang again. He looked, it was Bert Kling.

"You were right. We spotted Thompson mowing his wife's lawn about an hour ago. We're getting a warrant now, and we're going to hit the house at nine."

"OK, could you let me know when he's in custody? I'll probably have some questions for him. If you could ask them, I'd appreciate it. I'll probably be in Memphis by then."

"Roger that. Anything else?"

There wasn't. Jason rang off and focused on driving.

Jim hung up from Jason, and saw the text flash across his screen. He called back, and when Marianne answered he said, "Did they really say canoodling?"

Marianne laughed. "That's what they call it."

"Wow. What the hell does that even mean?"

"It's an ambiguous term. I think it means we were cuddling."

"OK. Do we do anything?"

"I can talk to my manager. I think for now the safest thing is to ignore it."

"Why not confirm it?"

"Wait, what?"

"Let's confirm it. I could not give a shit less what the press thinks, but why not tell them we're dating?"

"Really?"

"We'll tell them we've been dating for almost a month. That's not really a lie, and we can say we are taking it slow and seeing where it leads."

Marianne had a lump in her throat. "Are we? Taking it slow?"

"OK, that would be a lie. I'll talk to Hal, and he and Hank can put it out."

Marianne felt a little faint. "OK."

"You alright?"

"Never better. I'll see you when you get home."

She hung up before he had a chance to say anything else.

Lloyd and Ross were sitting at a computer, watching video and discussing the case.

"Mistaken identity?" Ross was curious.

"Consider it," said Lloyd. "Maybe he had the wrong room number."

"What about the wrong day?"

"What do you mean?"

"Maybe he's off by a week. Maybe she's coming next week."

"OK. But that's a really confused dude. I'll go talk to the manager."

"I'll go with you. I'm not getting anything here and I need a break."

At two on the nose, Jim and Captain Daniels walked into the conference room, along with captains from other investigative and administrative units. The chief hadn't shown up yet. As they sat down, Jims phone rang.

"Jim, you sure you want to announce a relationship?"

"Why not?"

"Jim, you have no idea the scrutiny you'll be under. The press can be really invasive."

"I have an idea about that. I gotta go, and Marianne?"

"What Jim?"

"I love you."

Jim hung up the phone.

"Who's Marianne," asked Captain Daniels.

The chief walked in, and Jim breathed out slowly.

"What did he say," said Jane.

"He said go ahead," Marianne said softly.

"That's it?"

"No. He said he loved me."

"Aw shit."

Marianne had a tear rolling down her cheek. Jane hugged her around the shoulders.

Jim and Captain Daniels walked out of the chiefs conference room. "Did you really just tell the chief that a and I quote, 'person of interest is on the lam?'"

"I believe I did. Stroke of genius on my part, if I do say so myself."

"What the hell? You looked like an idiot."

"Idiot savant maybe. They focused on that one expression so much that they forgot entirely about Jason being in Tennessee."

Captain Daniels let out a chuckle. "OK. You bought us some time. When do you expect to hear from him?"

"After he talks to detectives in Memphis. Probably around ten tomorrow."

51

He was sitting at a table in the Capitol Hill branch of the public library, scrolling through articles.

"Singer Marianne Wilson was spotted at The Lime in Kirkland last night. Witnesses said she was canoodling with local writer TW Griffin."

He had no idea who TW Griffin was. But he brought up a search engine, and typed in the name. The first article was a review of a book. It had mostly positive reviews and for a time had been in the top twenty five of best sellers. "Bullshit," he thought, but found a Wikipedia entry that showed TW Griffin was an "American author, that lives near Seattle, in the 'Hunts Point' neighborhood." A search for Hunts Point showed it to be an upper class neighborhood on the east side of Lake Washington.

"Well well well. I've still got time."

Chapter Nine

Jason was an hour out of Memphis when his phone rang again. He looked and saw it was Detective Kling.

"Jason, we got him," Bert said excitedly. "He was trying to haul his fat butt into the attic when we went in."

"Good. He say anything yet?"

"Not yet. We're taking him to headquarters. His wife is going too, for harboring. Plus she fought with us. Tried telling us the search was unconstitutional."

"Excellent. Hang on a second." Jason pulled to the side of the highway and turned on his flashers.

"I'll need to know when the last time he was in Seattle. Where was he on Saturday. Who can verify that. Then ask him his relationship with Abigail Dunbar. Find out what if any history there was. Also, I'll need witnesses that can back up anything he says. You may need to interview the ex separately. I doubt he ever left town."

"We'll try. He may lawyer up, but we'll try. If he talks, I'll send you the CD."

"OK. I'm almost to Memphis. If I need to come back, it'll have to be tomorrow."

"Don't sweat it."

Jason ended the call and followed the GPS in the car to a motel 6 on the edge of town.

Bert Kling rolled his head around his shoulders, then stretched his arms across his chest. He was thinking of his strategy and what Jason had said about Thompson being a "person of interest." He picked up two files and after making sure the recorders were running, walked into the interview room. His partner was watching through the one way window.

"Hi Arnie."

Thompson sat glumly in a chair at a long table, his wrists manacled to a ring in the middle.

"Do you watch the news, Arnie?" Bert was smiling and pleasant.

"No."

"I've been thinking about where I'm going to go on vacation this year. I just met a guy that came to town from Seattle. I'm thinking about going out there this summer. Have you ever been to Seattle, Arnie?"

"No."

"Really? That's odd." Bert opened a file and started scanning a piece of paper at the top. He looked up and said, "are you sure you were not in Seattle last Saturday?"

Arnie waved a hand, then said, "I was going to go but then all this other bullshit happened."

Bert had to be careful now. "Who went instead?"

"Abigail did. And probably a couple other guys."

"You had a thing for Abigail, didn't you?"

Arnie smiled, "Yeah man, she was gorgeous. But she was like the ice princess, you know? I could never get her to warm up man."

"Were you upset that she was getting your job?"

"I'm done there anyhow. I don't care who replaces me."

Bert sat on the table next to Arnie. "Arnie, you sure you weren't just a little mad at her?" He held his first two fingers about a quarter inch apart. "Just a little bit?"

"Maybe a little. But not really. I mean I don't want to lose the job but what the hell."

"Arnie, where were you on Saturday?"

"Man you know where I was. Stuck in my wife's house, listening to her bitch about all the trouble she was gonna be in."

Bert pulled a photo from the file. "Arnie, did you do this," he asked as he slid the photo in front of Arnie.

Thompson sat up with a jolt. "Holy shit!"

"Arnie?"

"Detective this is awful! I had nothing to do with this. What the hell?"

Bert let him ramble on for a couple of minutes, but his reaction told Bert everything he needed to know.

"OK, thanks Arnie. Oh, let me read you something," Bert said, as he picked up the second file.

Lloyd and Ross arrived back at the Olympus Hotel, and parked in the turn around. The manager recognized them and was most cooperative.

"That room was originally booked for a week. But she only stayed two nights."

"Is that unusual?"

"It happens. Not often, but it does. Usually they have to cut the trip short for some reason. In this case she didn't say. She ordered a car from the lobby, and left with all her bags. I assumed she was going to the airport."

"Abigail checked in Saturday afternoon. What time was the room vacated?"

"Around eleven in the morning I think. The room was made up within the hour."

"Thank you. Can we get a printout of the information?"

"The privacy of our guests…"

Lloyd interrupted him. "Do I need to remind you that this is a murder investigation? Imagine the damage this will cause your reputation if we have to tell the press that we couldn't catch the killer because you were all constipated about guest privacy."

"I was about to say the privacy of our guests is secondary to getting this dangerous criminal off the streets."

"That's what I thought you'd say."

Ross asked, "who was going to get the room after Ms Dunbar?"

"It doesn't work that way."

"What do you mean?"

"Let's say you reserve a room in advance. We know we will need X number of rooms due to reservations. So we make sure we rent out only enough rooms so we have plenty for the ones that are reserved. When you show up, we pull a room from the pool of reserved rooms. So basically we don't know which room you're going to be in until you walk up to the front desk."

"OK, thanks. Could I ask for a specific room?"

"You could," said the manager," but that doesn't happen very often. Usually, if it does, it's a couple trying to relive some kind of memory."

"Got it, thanks. Can you get that printout?"

As he was walking away, Lloyd said, "so it wasn't someone coming later. It had to be someone that just left."

Ross said, "so how would he know the room number?"

"I don't know. I've got to think on this."

Ross said, "Hang on a minute."

He went back to the manager and asked, "Who was on duty at the desk Friday night?"

He looked in the computer for a minute. "Rose Littlejohn."

"Is she here today?"

"No, she's off. She won't be in until later."

Lloyd looked at Ross, then said, "Thank you." The manager went back to the printer.

Ross said, "we need to talk to her."

Lloyd held his finger to his lips, and held up his smart phone. A white pages app showed Rose Littlejohn lived in an apartment off of 23rd avenue and E Yesler street. Ross nodded that he understood.

Five minutes later, Lloyd and Ross were walking out with more video and Cassidy Upton' name and address in Oklahoma.

Jim and his captain came into the bullpen. A few detectives were still at work, some typing up reports, others killing time. Captain Daniels followed Jim to his office, and inside, asked, "aren't you worried at all about the chief?"

"She will never admit that I got one over on her. By now she know's it, but she can't do anything about it. Jason is safe, and the city will cover him. We're going to come out of this looking good."

"What about your future? She could send you back to a precinct and put you in uniform."

"So what? If she does that, she knows it would hurt the department. She's got cover, and she wants to get this guy as bad as we do. If she really wanted to put me in uniform, she would have done so long ago. And even if she did, there are worse things."

Daniels wasn't so sure, but he didn't argue.

Jim closed out his computer, and stood to leave. Daniels was still in the doorway. He looked like he wanted to say something, but was having trouble sorting out the words.

"Bill, I'm telling you, we're good."

"If you say so. If you can't find this guy, it could all back fire on you."

"There are what, six million people in the Puget Sound region. Three million are women, so that leaves about three million men. Of those, about one point five million are white. Right there we've eliminated over four million suspects. At that pace, it won't be long."

Daniels shook his head. "Get him soon, Jim." Then he turned and walked out.

Jim took one last look at the file. "Not to worry," he said to himself. Then he walked out.

Jim walked to his car in the parking garage, then drove down and went out through the gate. He got into line with the cars headed to the 520 bridge. It was rush hour, and he was cursing his luck. And realizing how nervous he was. He had no idea what to expect when he got home. Had he driven her off? Would she be there? What the hell was the next step?

As soon as he got on the bridge, he could see an accident mid span that blocked the way. It wasn't terribly unusual, but today it chafed. Cars started driving around on the left side, so Jim eased into the left lane. He saw the troopers coming the wrong way on the highway and a tow truck right behind them. No ambulance, so that was good. One of the cars was a bronze van, the driver looking to be about eighty, yelling at a young woman in a newer Volkswagen. She was petrified, her windows rolled up and staring straight ahead. Just before he got up to the scene, the first of the troopers arrived, and the old man seemed to calm down. Jim squeezed around on the left and kept going.

He took his exit and spotted a road side stand selling flowers on the corner. He pulled up, and rolled down his window.

"You got any roses?"

"How many you want?"

"About a dozen. How much are they?"

"Depends. How much trouble are you in?"

Jim laughed, "I have no idea. I just think I need to be prepared."

"What did you do?"

"I told her I loved her."

"That ain't so bad."

"I don't think she was expecting it."

"I'll give you a discount," he said, "Forty bucks, man."

Jim handed him a fifty. "Keep the change."

"Good luck man. I hope she's worth it."

Jim drove into his neighborhood. He waved to the gate guard as he raised the barrier, and drove down his street. He backed into his garage, then took some deep breaths, waiting to get his emotions under control.

Jim swept the flowers off the seat next to him, squared up his shoulders and went into the house. The lights were dim. At first it was quiet, as he walked into the living room. Then from the dining room he heard the Turnpike Troubadors,

"And we're caught up in the riff-raff

Circling 'round the sun

It takes a lot of blood and tears just to really love someone…"

Jim walked slowly to the entrance, a lump in his throat. He stood in the doorway. The table was set with candles. A covered serving platter sat between two chairs. Wine had been poured. But he wasn't seeing that.

Marianne was standing by the table, dressed in a red and white wrap around dress that hugged her body. She was still holding the lighter, her blond hair cascading past her shoulders, green eyes bright.

"We have to have some rules."

"Yes ma'am."

"You never tell me you love me, without giving me a chance to say I love you back."

"Ok."

"I've drafted a release. I want you to read it before I give it to Hank."

"OK." Jim handed her the roses. She stepped past them and kissed Jim full on the mouth, a long, lingering kiss. "I love you," she said.

The stereo played:

"...I traveled round and I ain't found nobody quite like you
And is all this living meant to be or a happy accident?
But in my heart you pay no rent
Well in my heart you pay no rent..."

Chapter Ten
Wednesday

Jim woke up first. Marianne was laying with her head on his chest, breathing slowly. He reflected on the night before, and thought about the press release she had composed.

"Ms Wilson and TW Griffin are confirming that they have been dating for some time, and are in a committed relationship."

He thought it was fine. Succinct. To the point. He buried his nose in her hair and inhaled deeply.

"What are you doing?"

"Sorry honey, I thought you were asleep."

"I was dreaming I was an ant and you were an anteater," she said.

"I'll get coffee," he said, laughing as he slid out from under her.

He came back a few minutes later, and set her coffee on the nightstand. She sat up, revealing a silky white nightgown.

"How do you feel about hunting?"

"You mean finding animals in the woods, shooting them and then eating them? Or going out into the woods as an excuse to drink all night, sleep late, and buy a roast at Safeway?"

"Either one. I've got a couple horses I keep over near bridal trails. We could load them up and take them to my cabin this weekend."

"You had me at horses. I'll need a rifle and a hunting license."

"I've got a rifle you can use. And I'll pick up a deer tag today."

Jim was stepping into the shower. In three minutes, he was out, clean and shaved.

"How do you do that so quick?"

Jim shrugged.

"If all goes well, I'll be home on time tonight."

He kissed her and stepped out the door.

He was angry. No that wasn't right. He was raging. He could not believe it. That woman had caused the accident when she hit her brakes. That's why he was so angry. It was all her fault, but he got a ticket. He tried his breathing exercises to calm down. But the rage was still building. At least the trooper had helped him with the exchange of information. He'd been careful. He had a stolen drivers license just in case something like this happened. Then he realized. He could do her a favor by saving her soul and avenging the accident. He took the blade and carefully wrapped it. He looked at his watch, and decided he had just enough time.

When Jim walked through the bullpen, Lloyd and Ross were back at the computer typing up bulletins. Jim passed through, and went into his office. Just as he hung up his coat, his phone rang. A moment later, he came out, looked around and saw Lloyd and Ross.

"Murray, Nolan!" They looked up. "I need you to head over to Bellevue. They got a homicide over there. One of the detectives remembered reading about your murder, and thought it looked similar."

"So," asked Ross.

"I asked what was used, he said it was a dagger. The handle and pommel are formed by two snakes intertwined."

"Shit. It's a signature," shouted Lloyd. Jim gave them the address, and they grabbed their coats.

Lloyd led them to an unmarked Crown Victoria, while Ross brought up the address on his GPS. They dropped down to the exit, then headed for the freeway. Lloyd took them across I-90. The GPS took them east of the city, to the Sylvia apartments. They were decent enough but certainly closer to two stars than five.

Lloyd parked in the lot, along with a number of other police vehicles, most of which held Bellevue Police markings. They had a command post set up, with a converted RV. Lloyd and Ross were directed inside. There, they encountered the incident commander, a patrol captain in uniform, with skin the color of coffee. He introduced himself as Captain Blackwell. He introduced them to Detective Francis Marlon, the lead investigator and his partner, Detective Julie Macready.

"The call came in to patrol at about eight AM. The victim, Sarah Carter, was a nineteen year old student at the University of Washington. She was supposed to get a ride from a friend this morning, but when she didn't come out, her friend went up to check on her." As Francis talked they were walking up to the second floor apartment. "When he got to her door, he knocked, but no answer. So he opened it and found this." Marlon opened the door. Inside was a studio apartment. A bed was centered against the back wall. On it was a body, with a dagger protruding from her chest. Lloyd recognized it immediately.

"That's going to be number two in a set of six."

"What do you mean," asked Julie.

"It's identical to the blade in ours, except it's likely smaller. We've tracked it to a burglary in Memphis."

"We're a long ways from Memphis," said Francis.

"Close to 2400 miles."

"How did he get in," asked Ross.

"Not sure. No sign of forced entry."

"We have him on video, looks like he was picking the lock at our scene," said Ross.

"You got a picture?"

"No, he never looked at the camera."

"Bummer."

Lloyd asked, "The ride, is that a normal thing?"

"No," Marlon replied. "The friend said that she was in an accident yesterday, and didn't want to drive."

"Where's her car?"

"She got a rental yesterday, after her car was towed off the bridge. Her Volkswagen got hit pretty good, I guess."

"What about her," asked Lloyd.

"No injuries from the accident. Well, maybe a sore neck."

"Background," asked Ross.

Julie looked at her notes and said, "Apparently she had an, uh, active social life. No steady boyfriend but two or three she saw regularly."

"Where are they?"

"Two were in class this morning. One was at work, some kind of computer geek."

"She see any of them last night," asked Lloyd.

"No. She had a date with one of them, but she called him and broke it. Said she didn't feel well."

"You need anything from us?"

"Copy of your file?"

"Sure, we'll fax it over. Can you copy us in on yours?"

"You bet."

On the way back, Ross called Jim and briefed him.

"You say she was in an accident yesterday," Jim asked.

"On the 520 bridge. She got rear ended."

"Why don't you swing by the Roanoke state patrol office, see if you can get a copy of the report and see if the troopers have any camera footage."

"Marlon will probably do that."

"Tell him what you are doing, and make sure he gets a copy. But call him after. I want that video."

Ross hung up the phone and turned to Lloyd. "Do you think…"

"It's spring. There's a lot of romance in the air. Yeah, Francis and Julie are dating."

"I thought I was losing it. How will that affect their investigation?"

"Depends on them. You don't get to be hot shot homicide detectives without knowing how to be professional. So, it might be a benefit, actually."

Marianne made herself busy putting together her breakfast. Then she dressed, and walked up the street to Jane's. She let herself in, and found Jane in her office, typing on a computer. Jane waved her to a chair, and finished the document she was working on.

"Hey you."

"Jim wants to take me hunting."

"For how long?"

"He said Friday after he gets off work, come back on Sunday."

"Are you taking the horses?"

"Yes."

Jane smiled. "His hunting cabin is what you might call 'rustic.' No running water, no electricity. He has a hand pump that runs water into the sink, but you have to boil it before you drink it."

"I haven't done something like that since I was a kid."

"Sheridan and I spent a couple of days there last year. Oh, did I mention there is no cell phone reception?"

"Sounds perfect." Marianne held up her phone. "I'm getting sick of this thing."

"You'll need a sturdy pair of jeans and boots."

"I've got the boots. My jeans won't work on horses."

"Looks like we're going shopping."

Marianne raised her arms over her head, like she was signaling a touchdown.

He smiled as he watched the scene across the street. He had seen an old crown Victoria drive up, and two men in plainclothes get out. One was a large white guy, the other almost as big, but a black man. He'd saved this one. These two would know that. He started his van and drove towards Hunts Point.

Lloyd and Ross got back to the bullpen at two in the afternoon. Jim saw them coming in, and walked out to greet them.

"The trooper went home right after he wrote up that crash, and hasn't submitted his report or uploaded his video. The good news is that there is video. The sergeant there is trying to reach him."

"OK, that's something. I heard from Jason. There is a set of six knives. They range from sixteen inch blades to eight. The last one is a letter opener."

"Well, the sixteen inch was at our scene. The fourteen inch is probably at Bellevue's."

"There's four more blades out there. I really don't want four more bodies before we get this guy."

"Understood. Hey, can you approve another bulletin for me?"

"Sure, let me see it."

"As soon as I'm done with it. Give me a minute."

Jim went back to his office. Lloyd came in a few minutes later, holding a printout. Jim reached out and took it from him, without looking up. He set it on his desk before finishing an email. He scanned the first page then looked at the photograph.

Lloyd watched as Jim sat up. "What is this?"

"Another person of interest."

"She's not your suspect."

"Probably not. But even if she's not, she could be a witness."

"Based on what?"

"Jim, she was renting the room before Abigail Dunbar. She checked in using a fake drivers license from Oklahoma. The receptionist that was working Friday night said that an older white guy called asking for her but wouldn't leave a message. I need to know why, and she may be the key to finding our suspect, even if she's not…"

"Do not send this. Give me an hour."

"Lieutenant, what the hell…"

"I'll call you Lloyd."

Jim grabbed his coat and headed out the door, brushing past Sgt. Worthy as he went by. Lloyd followed him to the bullpen and let him go.

"Mike, something's off with the lieutenant."

"What do you mean, Lloyd."

"I showed him a flyer I wanted to put out. He told me no and ran out the door."

"Shit, he never says no. Did he say why?"

"No. He said he'd call me in an hour."

"Give him ten minutes. Then head to Hunts Point."

"Thanks."

"Hang back. If he needs back up he'll call you."

"Yes sir."

Jim got to his car, and climbed in. The world seemed to be moving all around him. He fumbled for his phone, dropped it, then caught it. He took a deep breath and let it out slowly. Things came back into focus for him, his mind suddenly sharp. He looked at his phone, and pushed a number on speed dial. It rang four times and the voice mail answered.

"Honey, call me back."

Jim started down the ramp, tires squealing as he went around the turns. The gate came up, and he pulled out onto sixth avenue, cut across the street, and cut through the parking lot under the freeway, getting himself onto the north bound on ramp. The light was red, but he hit his lights and siren, and cut through the light. He left them on going up the freeway, then cut over on 520 again, staying on the left, passing cars. He was focused and urgent, forcing himself to turn his head to keep track of the other drivers. Twice he hit his redial, but still no answer. Jim kept thinking of the line on the flier. "There is no PC for arrest, but she should be detained and detectives contacted." He took his exit, and cut his lights on the surface streets. Driving well above the legal limits, he arrived at the gates of his neighborhood in just under ten minutes. The guard raised the gate, and he drove through, a little faster than his homeowners association allowed. Jim left his car in the driveway, at an angle. Surveying the house,

64

nothing seemed out of place. Jim walked swiftly to the front door. He stood off to the side, and ran his thumb across the sensor. The lock released, and he slowly pushed the door open. He drew his gun, and took a small flashlight off his belt.

Stepping over the threshold his senses were on high. The lights were on in the kitchen, but there was no sound. Jim made a decision and headed up the stairs, away from the kitchen but towards the bedrooms calling for Marianne as he went. He looked down the hallway. All the doors were closed, including the main bedroom. Slowly he pushed the door open, and followed his gun into the darkened bedroom.

Across the room was a man holding a gun, aimed at him. Startled, Jim took a step back, aiming for the chest area. The man took a step back. Jim let his finger off the trigger, and shined his light. The man shined a light at him. Jim realized he'd been holding his breath, and turned on the bedroom light. He had been about to shoot his reflection in a full length mirror.

He heard the door open downstairs.

"Jim, are you home?" Marianne's voice sounded melodious.

"I'll be right down." Jim put his Glock away with shaking hands, and slid the flashlight back onto his belt.

"I'm in the living room. You left your car out front." Jim came into the living room and kissed her on the lips.

"Get a room," said Jane.

"You guys were shopping, I see."

"I needed a few things for this weekend. Jim, what's going on?" Marianne had seen the look on Jims face.

"We have a problem." Jim produced the flier from his coat pocket. Marianne looked at it, then took a second, closer look.

"Well shit."

"I had no idea you were at the Olympus before you came here. But Lloyd is going to need to talk to Cassidy Upton."

"This is about the murder?" Jim nodded. "Honey, I've been with you all weekend."

"I may be wrong, but I seriously doubt he thinks you're a suspect. My best guess is Lloyd is on his way out here to talk to you. He's been working a theory that Abigail was not the intended target. I told him I'd call in an hour, but knowing him…". Jim let the sentence hang.

"I'll get Cassidy on. Jim, It'll take a few minutes."

"I'll help," said Jane. "Does she need a lawyer?"

"Let's leave lawyers out of it for right now. I'll sit with her. I really don't think she has any legal bullshit to worry about."

"Jim," Jane said, "Marianne is not your ordinary 'person of interest.' If the media gets wind of this..."

"Hold that thought," interrupted Jim. "She's not a suspect. Lloyd even said she might be a witness. And if the media gets wind of this then we spin it that she's cooperative and assisting in the investigation."

"Mm hmm." Jane was not convinced.

The women went upstairs. Jim breathed again, feeling like the first time in hours. He pulled his phone from his pocket and dialed Lloyds number. Lloyd answered on the first ring.

"I've been wondering what the hell is going on, lieutenant."

"Lloyd, where are you?"

"I'm sitting at the gates to this neighborhood, wondering how a simple policeman like yourself can afford to live here."

"I am fortunate enough to have good friends, Lloyd. When you come through the gate, take the first right, and follow it until you see my patrol car in the driveway. Put the guard on, he'll let you in."

Lloyd passed the phone to the guard, who spoke briefly with Jim, then smiled and handed the phone back. He told Lloyd, "I appreciate your understanding sir. I hope you can understand my situation."

Lloyd nodded, and drove through the gate. He followed the directions, locating Jims patrol car still creaking as it cooled. Ross sat beside him, silent. They parked behind Jims car, effectively blocking it in. Lloyd was wary, and his boss was acting strangely. They got out of the car, and walked warily to the front door. Before they could knock, Jim opened it from the inside.

"Come in. Coffees on."

Lloyd and Ross followed Jim into the dining area. Jane set out five cups. They could hear coffee sputtering into a carafe.

"You don't have to be here for this," Jim said.

"Among my many talents is that I have a law degree, and have duly passed the bar in the state of Washington. It has been a while since I've worked as a lawyer, and I'm more of a business law type, but I believe I know enough to get by."

"OK, you can stay," said Jim.

Marianne came down the stairs. She was dressed in a white sleeveless blouse and jeans, a string of pearls around her neck. She was carrying a paper bag.

"Lloyd, this is Cassidy Upton," Jim said.

"No offense, but you don't look like her," said Lloyd.

"No, I don't suppose I do," said Marianne. She walked to the table and upended the bag on it. The wig, glasses and prosthetic teeth landed on the table. The glasses landed on the wig, and the teeth fell off onto the floor. "This is Cassidy Upton."

"I'm afraid I don't understand," Lloyd said.

"When I travel I sometimes put this on and go by that name. I've made a couple albums that have done really very well, and I'm very thankful, but sometimes the recognition gets to be a little much."

"OK. I'm just going to dive right in. How do you know Abigail Dunbar?"

"I don't. I never heard the name until Jim told me about her."

"How about Alan Dunbar?"

"I don't know him either." Her tone was clipped and terse.

"How long have you and Lieutenant Churchill been seeing each other?"

Marianne looked thoughtful. "We've been dating for a little while now."

Lloyd nodded. "Who's TW Griffin? My wife tells me that you just announced a relationship with him."

Jim chimed in, "Lloyd, this house is owned by TW Griffin."

Lloyd shot Jim a look, then said to Marianne, "is that true? You're dating Jim and Mr. Griffin?"

"Just Jim."

"OK. When did you get in to Seattle?"

"Thursday. I flew in through SeaTac airport and took a taxi to the hotel. I checked in as Cassidy, with an Oklahoma license that is fake. I do that to avoid trouble."

"When did you check out?"

"Saturday morning. Friday I did some shopping and took in the sights. I had dinner at the Space Needle with my agent. I got back to the hotel around seven. On Saturday I checked out around ten, and took an Uber out here."

"What's the purpose of your trip?"

"Mr. Griffin's agent has asked me to perform some music for a movie that he's making. I came out to talk to him and get a feel for the project."

"OK. What would you say if I told you that we think you were the intended target?"

"I would say that sounds pretty awful," Marianne said.

"If you were the intended victim, do you have any thoughts as to who would want to hurt you?"

"I get all kinds of letters, and some are pretty hateful. But no one stands out."

"Ma'am, I have to ask some hard questions. It might be better if Jim wasn't here."

"We have no secrets," said Marianne. She reached over and took Jims hand."

"OK. You went through a pretty ugly divorce a couple years ago."

"It was bad," she acknowledged.

"You're ex has said some pretty rough things."

"He may have started a rumor that I had an affair while we were still married."

"Has he ever threatened you?"

Marianne hesitated. "Once."

"What happened?"

"He came in drunk. Called me some names and threw me up against a wall like I was a rag doll. When he let me go, I went and got my gun. I locked myself in my room until he passed out. Then I packed a bag and left."

"And this was in Stillwater?"

"Oklahoma, yes."

"Did he ever threaten you after that?"

"I drove all night to get to Amarillo. He didn't call until he came to in the morning. I told him that if he showed up in Amarillo, I would shoot him on sight."

"And he backed down?"

"Underneath it all he really is just a coward."

They talked for about an hour, Jim and Marianne holding hands. At the end of it, Lloyd said to Jim, "It's probably best if you aren't involved in the case anymore."

"Fuck that. I'm still your boss until someone decides I'm not."

"Jim…" Ross started.

"This is your case. If you develop information that someone I'm close to may be a suspect, give it to Daniels. Or Worthy. This is one of those unfortunate coincidences."

"There's the question of security for Ms Wilson."

"Please, call me Marianne," she said sweetly.

"This is a gated community. The house here is alarmed. Marianne and I will make whatever security arrangements we need to make."

Lloyd paused for a moment, his eyes fixed on the ceiling.

"I guess you're safe enough with him," Lloyd said, "I think we've covered everything. Marianne, do you have any questions for us?"

Marianne was quiet for a moment, then asked, "are you saying that Abigail Dunbar is dead because of me?"

"No ma'am. She's dead because some asshole killed her. We don't know what the motivation was, but it looks like he's killed again and we want to stop him before anyone else gets hurt."

Jim walked Lloyd and Ross to the door.

"Jim, I can keep a lid on this for a while, but eventually.."

"I know Lloyd. I'll deal with what ever fall out comes, but we have to find this guy."

Ross said, "It could be somebody she knows."

"Or a deranged fan," said Lloyd.

"It could still be random, but I guess that doesn't help us much." Jims phone started to ring. "It's Jason," he said, pushing the answer button.

Jason had gone in to the Memphis Police headquarters and had promptly been directed to the Mt. Moriah station where he met detective Billy Holiday. Detective Holiday looked up the file, and found the burglar was a fourteen year old, who left his fingerprints all over the house. There was a delay in reporting because the homeowners were on vacation, but the knife set was a one of a kind. Detective Holiday had a message from a pawn shop that had sold the knives when they weren't claimed.

"Did you get surveillance video?"

"Does a bear shit in the woods," detective Holiday remarked.

Jason had viewed the video. It was an old man shuffling in. He'd gone straight to the knives and purchased the whole set at once. The video was a little blurry, but he thought the video techs at home could help with that. Then he called Lt. Churchill.

"I sent the video as an attachment to an email. I copied you in on the email, but it's blurry. I'm hoping Lloyd or Ross can get something out of it at the video unit."

"Good work Jason. When are you coming home?"

"As soon as I can get to the airport, I'll be on the next flight."

"Alright. See you at the office."

To Lloyd and Ross Jim said, "see what you can do with that video."

"Jim," said Lloyd, "One other thing."

"Go ahead."

Lloyd looked around. Ross looked at him, and started walking for the car. Lloyd stepped in close to Jim.

"Jim, I'm going to tell you this as a friend." Lloyd's voice was quiet. "I shouldn't have to remind you but this is a fucking murder investigation. Two people are dead so far and twice you have sat on information that could be vital. You'd better be straight with me or I will come after you. Friend or not, if you fuck up my investigation I will be all over you."

Jim's eyes turned dark and cold and he held Lloyd's gaze for a moment before they softened.

"OK, point made," he said, "there is one other thing."

Lloyd made a go ahead motion.

"Marianne is telling the truth about dating only me. But I've written a couple books under the name of TW Griffin."

"So you knew that producer?"

"I met him for the first time on Saturday. I pegged him as an asshole the minute I saw him. When I saw your flier I tried calling you but you didn't answer. So I hooked up with Ross at the hotel."

"What did you hear at the door?"

"Do I need a union rep?"

"Lieutenant it's just me. I want to know what you heard."

"Fine. She was crying. A little girl kind of cry and she was saying I don't want to. And I heard him say it was for a part." Jim was quiet for a minute, then, "that's the truth and that's what I'll be testifying to."

"What if you'd been by yourself? Would you have killed him," asked Lloyd.

"I guess we'll never know," said Jim. His eyes had turned cold and hard again. They looked at each other for another minute, then Jim turned and went inside, letting the door close behind him.

Jane and Marianne were still sitting at the dining room table. No one said anything as Jim walked back into the room. Jim opened the liquor cabinet and got out glasses, ice and a bottle of Jamesons. He poured a measure in each, and then walked the glasses to the table, handing one first to Marianne, then to Jane. Then he winked at the women, and took a strong pull. Jane took a sip. Marianne stirred the ice with her finger. Finally she took a sip, then looked at Jim.

"What happens now?"

"What do you mean?"

"This is going to come out. I can find another alias to travel under. But the world is going to know who you are now."

"For now, nothing. No one is going to know anything unless this goes to trial. But if I have to, I'll quit. Probably should have by now, anyway."

"Jim, you're good at what you do. Your people respect you. I could see that, even though I was pissed we had to go through it."

"One thing at a time. First we get this guy off the street. Then we worry about stuff that hasn't happened yet."

Jane nodded, and took another sip. "I think that's right. You've got money, and for reasons I cannot understand, it continues to roll in. If you're careful you would never have to work again."

"All right then. Money's no problem. But, who needs money when you have love?"

"Oh dammit, Jim," exclaimed Marianne.

He had seen the Crown Victoria drive through the neighborhood, but he didn't follow it. Wherever they went, it was probably gated. He had to think about that. His van was leaking oil now. He would have to do something about that.

He pulled the dagger from it's place, and ran a hand over the blade. It was beautiful, and it was blessed. But he was running out of time. Two more days was all he had. Unless he could think of a way to get more time.

Chapter Eleven
Thursday

Jason stepped off the plane. He'd spent the last seven hours on the flight and felt it. He was bleary eyed and unshaven and it was two in the morning. He retrieved his car from the parking garage, billing the city yet again for the expense. With no where else to go, he headed up the freeway to his office. Once there, he retrieved his Dopp kit from his locker, then showered and shaved. He retrieved a relatively fresh shirt and pants from his duffel bag, and put them on, securing his gun on his hip. Then he went to his desk, and checked his email. He found the video, and watched it again. An old man going into a Memphis pawn shop. Making a purchase, then leaving again. His face wasn't clear, but he was certain the video unit could clean it up.

He poured a cup of coffee, then went to his desk and began typing up his reports for the last few days. He sent Lieutenant Churchill a text message. "I'm back. In the office." He got a response almost immediately. "Trooper should be coming by with another video around six or seven. If I'm not there, take a look and see what you think." Jason looked at his watch and realized it was four in the morning.

Jim was staring at the ceiling. Marianne lay next to him, eyes closed, breathing softly. Jason' message alerted him, but he had mostly been dozing. He realized, not for the first time, how much he liked watching Marianne sleep. As quietly as he could, he slid out of bed and went to shower. After his customary three minutes, Jim had dressed in slacks and a shirt, open neck, no collar. Marianne sat up, and blinked.

"Hi."

He bent and kissed her. "Hi honey. Wait here, I'll get coffee."

He was back in less then five minutes. Marianne hadn't moved. She sat up and took her coffee, holding it in both hands and smelling the steam as it drifted towards the ceiling.

"How much time do you have," she asked.

"All the time in the world."

"You haven't asked me about what happened with Brian."

Brian was her ex-husband.

"I'm here if you want to talk. I didn't ask because it wasn't my business. All that is before we met. But hey, I watch TMZ sometimes."

She smiled wryly. "Even at the worst of it, I was always loyal. But I knew if I didn't draw the line it would get worse."

Jim took her hand. "I'm glad you did. When I met you in person, it was like I'd known you forever." He paused for a moment. "Do you think…"

"No," she said. "Not really. If he was drunk, maybe. But when he sobers up he's ok. But. He was coming home drunk every night."

He stroked her cheek and kissed her gently. "I'm worried about leaving you here alone."

"I'll be ok. Jane is going to her office today. I'll be fine here."

"You could come to work with me."

She cupped his face in her hands. "Jim, it's sweet that you're worried about me. But I'll be fine. I have my pistol if I need it."

"Make sure you carry it with you at all times then."

"Jim, I'll be fine."

Jim nodded and kissed her. Then he went downstairs and was gone.

Marianne drained her coffee and looked at the clock. "I can't believe he gets up that early," she said to herself. She showered and toweled herself dry, then on a whim, shaved her legs. She checked herself out in the mirror and liked what she saw. Then she got dressed in her favorite t shirt and her torn jeans and walked out of the bedroom. She realized that she had never walked through the house. The first bedroom had it's own bathroom, back to back with the master bath, she found. The next two were straightforward bedrooms, with closets. The last one she found had been converted to an office. It ran the width of the house, and was almost as big as the master bedroom, except that it did not have a bathroom and the closet was not a walk in. A window overlooked the lake to the west. To the east was the street. South were trees, and probably the next door neighbors. On the wall were several certificates. She looked over the various awards. On the desk, was a note pad and a telephone alongside a new Macintosh computer. Otherwise the desk itself was bare. On the walls were paintings of local mountains, but this was a room strictly for working. Marianne noticed a calendar on the wall and some pictures of what looked like family. There were none of his wife. She felt a little guilty and left, closing the door behind her.

Marianne went downstairs and made a light breakfast, then headed to the basement. She liked the music room, even if a bit spartan. Maybe if she was going to be here a while she'd do something about that. She stepped inside, and put her some music on a stand, then slipped on some headphones and picked up the guitar. She made some adjustments to tune it, and strummed it. She ran through some scales and then began singing.

Jim walked into the bullpen an hour later. Lloyd and Ross were talking to Jason, and looking at something on the computer.

"What do you have?"

Lloyd glanced at Ross, and then said, "we were filling in Jason, and checking out state patrol's video."

"Where did you leave off?"

Ross said, "We were just telling him how we interviewed Marianne Wilson for this case."

"What's on the video," said Jim.

Jason chimed in. "It's the in car video from the collision on 520 the other day. Check this out."

He scrolled back, and ran the video forward. An old man was berating the trooper.

"Look at the hoody," Ross said. The hoody the old man was wearing was old and worn.

"Looks like the same hoody from the hotel, but there must be a few million like it out there."

"True, but he had a fake drivers license."

"Didn't the trooper check it?"

"Yes, but it came back clear. Good address and everything. But the address would put it in the middle of Greenlake, and the owner of the drivers license was killed in Vietnam during the Tet Offensive."

"No shit? This could be our guy. Jason, anything off the Memphis video?"

"I'm seeing if the video unit can clean it up. Here's the original." Jason made a couple clicks of the mouse key, and another video crowded out the troopers video. "It looks like him, but I can't be sure."

"No bulletins, until we know for sure."

"OK."

"Can you print me out a still from the troopers video?"

"Sure boss. Why?"

"I want to show it to someone later."

Jason printed it out, and handed it to Jim, who slid it into his notebook.

The phone rang at Sgt. Worthy's desk. He came out a moment later and announced, "shooting in Greek row."

Jason said, "Fred and I are up."

Ross and Lloyd volunteered to go. Jim looked at his office and then turned and headed for the door.

Twenty minutes later, they were being briefed at the command post. The patrol sergeant, whom Jim thought looked like he was about twelve, told them, "the victim was walking north on 17th. The suspect stepped out from the driveway, and fired one round, striking the victim in the forehead. He was dead when he hit the ground."

"What about the shooter," asked Jason.

"He ran back down the driveway and into the house."

The house was a fraternity. Jim hadn't been inside in a long time, but knew that they were a rabbit warren of rooms. "He's in there?"

"Yes sir."

"It could take days to get him out, if he didn't run out the back."

"People coming out said no one went upstairs. Two guys said he went downstairs."

Lloyd and Jason both said at the same time, "Chapter room."

The sergeant said, "What?"

Jason explained, "Every fraternity has a chapter room. Sometimes the entrance is not visible unless you know where it is."

The young sergeant spoke into his radio, and soon a twenty something came up to the command post.

"How do you get into the chapter room," the sergeant asked.

"What do you mean?"

"Son, we are not interested in what you do in there. But you may have a murderer hiding inside that room."

Jim suppressed a chuckle. The sergeant didn't look any older than the fraternity kid.

The kid thought for a minute, then said, "I know it sounds cheesy, but there are two lights mounted on the wall. Pull them both at the same time."

The SWAT commander stepped in. "We'll need to put together a plan." The patrol lieutenant that was serving as the incident commander agreed, saying, "We'll try to hail him first."

About thirty minutes later, the plan was in place, and the SWAT team moved up behind ballistic shields. They spent ten minutes trying to call out to the suspect through the wall. When there was no answer, two SWAT officers on either side of the entry pulled the lights. When the door opened, another SWAT officer threw a flash bang grenade into the room.

When they went in, the suspect lay on a couch against the back wall. He'd put his gun in his mouth and pulled the trigger. Jim and Lloyd quietly agreed he'd probably been dead about an hour.

They left Jason and Fred at the scene to sort it out. Jason thought it was not random, that the suspect and victim had known each other. "I don't know how far this goes. We'll get warrants for his phone and computer history."

"Your suspect is dead. There won't be a prosecution," Jim said.

"All due respect sir, we don't know if anyone else is involved. This is a fraternity. If he's not a member he has to know someone that is."

"OK. Get the warrants. I'm headed back to the office. I'll get you a statement. Do you need Lloyd and Ross here?"

"No, I'm good."

Sergeant Worthy stayed behind. Jim, Lloyd and Ross headed back to the office.

At the office, the admin handed Lloyd a note. He read it and showed it to Jim. It read; "having difficulty with formatting. Am sending to state. Should be back by tomorrow." It was signed "Kim." Jim let out a profanity.

"Jim, I'm sure it's him. Why don't I release the BOLO?"

Jim sighed. "Because it's Bellevue's case. What we should be doing is forming a task force."

"Ross and I will be your task force."

Jim laughed, his tension easing. He went into his office and wrote out his statement. He came out, looked at Lloyd and Ross, and said, "How late are you guys working?"

Ross answered, "we decided to review the entire case file, especially after the interview yesterday. And we are going to review the video from the hotel. I think we missed something."

Lloyd stood up, and looked around the bullpen. There was no one else there. "How's Marianne?"

"She's holding up better than me. She was upset last night, but we talked some this morning."

Jim snapped his fingers, "I meant to tell you. Take a look at Brian, her ex. Just see if you can nail down his whereabouts. I think he may have been worse than she let on."

Lloyd said, "Way ahead of you." He clicked on his computer, and a video popped up. It was Brian singing at a concert. "This was taken

Saturday night in Lexington Kentucky. While Abigail was being murdered, Brian was almost three thousand miles away."

"Good work. I don't know how I feel about it, but thanks."

It took Jim just under twenty minutes to drive home. He slid his thumb across the sensor and heard the satisfying click of the door unlocking. He walked in, and said, "Marianne?" There was no answer. Jim walked into the living room, and saw the door to the deck was open. He looked outside, and saw Marianne, stretched out on a towel trying to catch the afternoon suns' rays. She was wearing the bottom half of a peach colored bikini. The top half was still tied around her neck, but she'd untied the lower string and it was stretched out underneath her. Jim stepped out on the deck and admired her backside for a moment, then called softly, "Marianne?"

"You're staring at my ass again, aren't you?"

"I plead nolo contendere your honor."

She reached underneath her and pulled the top into place. "Tie it for me please."

Jim knelt next to her and reluctantly tied the string into place. "This must have been expensive. There isn't much material."

"It's a designer, " she said as she got to her knees and shook her hair back into place. She squatted back on her ankles. "How was work?"

He told her. When he was finished, she said, "that's terrible. Why would someone do that?"

"Jason said it was over a woman. She'd broke up with one guy and was dating another. He couldn't deal with it."

"That's just so sad."

"Yep." He was sitting on the edge of a deck chair. "If we are going away for the weekend, we need to get some groceries."

"It intrigues me that you can talk about death so easily and then talk about eating."

"Part of it is being in this job so long. The other part is that I've been alone for so long."

"Well, you don't have to be alone now," she said. Marianne slid on a pair of cutoff jeans.

"If this trip is supposed to be about hunting, " she said, "I need a rifle."

"Come with me."

He took her by the hand and they went downstairs. In the safe room, Jim punched in a code from memory, then turned the handle and opened the door. Inside was a collection of rifles and pistols.

"Take your pick."

She looked over the guns for a moment, then came out with an AR-15. "What's this?"

"Not a bad choice, so long as the deer are shooting back."

She giggled and put it back, then pulled out a Henry 30-30. She opened the action, to make sure it was unloaded, closed it, and put it to her shoulder. She picked out an imaginary spot on the wall, put the rifle on her shoulder and pulled the trigger. There was a good crisp snap as the firing pin hit nothing but air.

"I like this one. It has a good feel."

"That's a good choice." Jim reached in and brought out a Weatherby Vangaurd out of the safe. "This is generally my go to for deer hunting." Jim grabbed a couple boxes of ammunition for each rifle, and placed them into hard sided cases that were stacked against the wall. "There's a good place to zero them near the cabin."

They took the cases upstairs, and stacked them against the wall of the bedroom. Jim changed into jeans and a flannel shirt while Marianne pulled a t shirt over her bikini top and stepped into a pair of sneakers.

"I don't know about wearing Cassidy."

"A couple things that people don't think about. A minor change in appearance is generally enough to throw people off. The glasses that you wore yesterday would be enough. People are used to seeing you with your hair down, so pull it back into a pony tail. That should be good. And if someone says that you look like Marianne Wilson, just say, 'oh, I get that all the time.'"

"You think that would work?"

"I throw on a pair of tinted glasses to be TW Griffin. No one has mistaken Jim Churchill for TW."

"OK, I'll try it."

They went downstairs again, and got into Jims Subaru. Jim drove to Safeway, and they went in holding hands.

He was careful. He had bought a sandwich in the deli, when he saw them walk in, hand in hand. Her hair was different, and she had the glasses on, but he would have known her anywhere. They were holding hands and talking quietly to each other. He looked away so as not to draw attention to himself. He was fuming. She was so close, but he did not like the look of that guy. He didn't look like any writer. His face had a hardness to it, he couldn't explain. And cruel eyes. He realized for the first time he was afraid. He went out to the parking lot, and got into his van. At that moment, he realized-that was the policeman in the explorer, the one from the Olympus. He drove out of the lot, and pulled into an auto parts store. They'd have to drive right by here.

Jim and Marianne left the store with their purchases. They loaded them into the back of his car, and closed it, then drove back to the house. Marianne saw Jim check his mirror and asked, "Something wrong?"

"Probably nothing. Thought I saw something.'

"Jim, I have something to tell you."

"What is it?"

"I went into your office today."

Jim tensed. "Did you go into the desk?"

"No."

Jim relaxed a little. "No problem."

"I was wondering what she looked like."

"Who?"

"Your wife."

Jim glanced at her. He thought about it for a moment, and then, "I guess I should tell you the truth."

Marianne was quiet.

He waited for the gate to come up, and after they went inside he said, "She was killed by a drunk driver." He paused, then said, " It was a one car crash."

"You mean you…"

"No. She was alone in the car."

"Oh my god. I'm so sorry, Jim."

"We'd been married for about four years. She was an alcoholic, or became one after we were married. Eventually, she became the disease. Everything became about getting the next drink. I couldn't handle it anymore so I left. We'd been separated about six months and I had just filed for divorce when the accident happened."

They pulled into the garage, and unloaded the car in silence. They dropped the bags in the kitchen, and Jim said, "Come upstairs for a minute."

They went down the hall to his office, and Jim went to his desk. He opened a drawer on the lower right, and pulled out a file.

"This might be pretty rough. The report is on top. Photo's are in the back." He left the file on his desk, and went downstairs.

Marianne opened the folder. The initial report was just two pages. Most of it was taken up with basic information about the driver and the car. Where there was supposed to be a diagram was a notation to "see attached sketch sheet." The narrative was brief. 'Vehicle one was southbound Aurora Ave at a high rate of speed. For unknown reasons vehicle one left the road and struck a telephone pole in the 4700 block. Detectives responded.'

Marianne flipped the page and saw the sketch sheet. The next page was detective notes. There was an indication that Heather had been drinking. Her blood alcohol was listed as '.032.' Marianne wasn't sure what that meant but was pretty sure that it was high. She saw a note that there were no skid marks. One witness said she had been, "driving like a bat out of hell." There were measurements and data that were mostly meaningless to her but by the time she read that the damage to the car and the pole were 'extensive' she knew that the detectives were able to verify the speed.

The pictures in the back were worse. The front of the car had a deep V going back almost to the windshield. The pole itself had sheared off at the base after it had done it's damage to the car. The windshield was missing. She knew from the report that it had been removed by firefighters trying to access Heather. They had tried desperately but had finally had to admit that their efforts were futile. The drivers door had been pried open and lay against the front fender. The roof had been pried up and bent in half over the back seat. Her body had still been inside, trapped by parts of the car. It had taken hours to pull the car apart enough to get her out.

Marianne slid the pictures and the report back in the file and leaned back in the chair to compose herself. She put the file back in the drawer and stood up.

Jim was in the kitchen sorting bags of food into meals for two for two nights. His back was to her when Marianne walked into the room.

"Jim, I'm sorry."

He continued sorting, so she said, "Did you talk to anyone about this?"

"I saw a shrink once a week or so for a year." His voice was flat and emotionless.

"Did it help?"

"Some. He said I had what he called survivors guilt. Where someone dies and another one lives. Only in my case it was because I thought if I'd been with her it wouldn't have happened."

"Why would you think that?"

Jim turned. His voice was still flat, but his eyes betrayed incredible sadness.

"Did you notice anything in the report?"

"There was a lot of data that I didn't understand. But I got she was speeding."

"What did you notice about skid marks?"

"There weren't any. Why is that?"

"There were two theories. One is that she was drunk and didn't realize how fast she was going."

"What's the other?"

"That she did it on purpose."

"Jim, I…". She stopped. "I don't know what to say."

"No one does. Hell, I don't. It was ten years ago and I still wonder if she did it on purpose or not."

Marianne paused for a minute. She looked Jim directly in the eye and said, "Even if she did commit suicide, you know it wasn't your fault, right?"

Jim blinked and pointed at his temple. "I know that here." He pointed at his chest. "But in here it took a while to accept that."

"So why are you telling me?"

Jim paused to gather his thoughts.

"I like having you around. This shouldn't be between us."

He'd followed them until he saw them turn into the gate. Then he just kept going. He drove around the point until he came back to the main road, south of the turn, and kept going south. He drove to the Kirkland public library and found an open computer. It took him a moment, but he found a real estate web site that listed the homes in the area, including partial names of the owners. The last names were blocked out. He started on the waterfront houses. He found one for Sheridan, but he had no idea who that was. Next door to it was a somewhat smaller house, owned by "James." None of the houses he clicked on had a "TW." A few had names that started with T, and one was TS, but that was it.

He leaned back in his chair for a moment, and closed his eyes. Then it hit him. When he'd seen him before, at the Hotel, he'd been driving a different car. He was driving a Ford then. And he was a cop.

He had a plan. He would wait until tonight, and strike when she was alone. It would be easy enough. He'd chosen carefully. It would be a sacrifice, but it would be worth it. Carefully he laid out the dagger. This was the third longest. He'd planned carefully and knew how to get in without being seen. And how to get out again.

Chapter Twelve
Thursday night.

He had found her house. He drove past it, then took a left, and then another and parked on the wrong side of the street. He put his hood up, and got out of the van, then walked slowly back the way he'd come. The street was quiet. He could hear cars on the highway, some distance off.

The house was dark and quiet. The car was there, so he knew she was home. The front porch was screened from the street, but no one was out anyway. The door was locked. Cautiously he got down on one knee, and pulled his picks from his pocket. The right one was on top. He worked the lock for a moment, then heard an audible click. He waited a moment, but there was no change inside. None of the lights came on. No dogs barking, no sense of alarm. He eased the door open just enough to slip inside. Gently he made his way to the bedroom. The door was closed but yielded under his touch. He drew the dagger from under his belt and looked in. She was asleep, blond curls cascading over the pillow. With eager anticipation, he licked his lips and headed for the bed. He raised his hands to chest level, and closed his eyes for a moment of quiet prayer, and then all hell broke loose.

From behind him, he heard, "What the hell?" He spun, stabbing instinctively with the dagger in a wild arc. It caught the man in the neck, completely by surprise. The man staggered backwards, clawing at the dagger. Oddly, he noticed this guy was wearing only boxer shorts. In shock from the surprise he was fixated on this guy, wondering what he was going to do now, when he heard a "boom" from behind him, and felt something slap his side, just under his right arm. Without thinking he sprinted out of the room, running for the front door, tensing for the next shot. He went out the door, but instead of running straight off the porch, he turned to his right just as another shot whistled past his head. He ran to the end of the deck, and vaulted the railing. He landed oddly, his left leg collapsing under him. He rolled to his feet and almost fell again. Half running, half limping he ran through the yards and then cut across the street. Then he went up to the next corner and up to his van. He jumped in, and started the van. Then he took a deep breath, trying to ease his trembling before easing away from the curb. Somehow he made it out to Aurora Ave, and went south. He found an empty space in front of a restaurant called 'Beth's Café.' The light was decent enough. He lifted up his hoody and his shirt, and looked at the wound. It was raw and ugly and blood had soaked his hoody and run down into his jeans, but it looked like a surface wound. He reached under the passenger seat and pulled out an ancient first aid kit. He located a bottle of iodine that was at least five years out of date. He shrugged, figuring it couldn't hurt. He dumped some onto a big gauze pad, and tried to clean up the wound as best he could. Then he got another gauze pad, and dumped more iodine onto it. With his left hand he held it onto his right side, while he dug out an old, brownish roll of adhesive tape. Somehow he managed to tape the pad on. When he took his hand away the pad was already soaked through with blood. He pulled two more pads from the box, and taped them over the first one.

"That'll have to do," he said to himself, and pulled his hoody down over the wound. He fingered the hole the bullet had left. Then he remembered his mission, got behind the wheel again and started driving.

He drove around the south end of Greenlake and somehow found himself on 45th, headed for the freeway along with what little traffic there was. He was confident he had eluded capture. From the other direction came a police car, lights flashing and siren blaring. He stared straight ahead as the cop passed him going the other way. He made it to the freeway and headed for 520. He thought of it as a bad luck bridge, but hoped he would be ok.

With the stop and dressing his wound it took him longer than he had planned. But as he drove across the bridge, he saw a dark blue Explorer going the other way, grill lights flashing and a siren blaring. He smiled to himself. Maybe his luck was turning.

He made it into Hunts Point, and parked the van off the street in a gas station lot, where he hoped no one would pay any attention to it. He grabbed his bag, and grimacing with the strain on his side, hoofed it the two blocks. He had noticed on the homes for sale site that this house seemed vacant. The back yard had a gate. He had marked it with a cone at the curb. Now he found the cone, and then the gate in the dark. He did not dare risk a light.

The gate was locked with a deadbolt. He wouldn't need his lock set for this. He pulled a screwdriver from the bag, and used it to push the deadbolt back. He eased in and closed and locked the gate. The grass was longer than he would have expected, although it did look evenly cut. He eased up to the house and peered through a window. A vacant living room stared back. "Perfect," he thought. He eased around to the front, and lay under the shrubbery. The entry to the neighborhood came in from the right. He unrolled a dark brown sleeping bag and crawled into it. Under the shrubbery he was virtually invisible. Then, he fell asleep.

Chapter Thirteen
Friday

It was just after midnight when Jims phone rang. Marianne said, "Again?"

Jim answered it, and listened quietly for a few minutes, asking occasional questions. When he hung up, Marianne asked, "Is it him again?"

Jim said, "Not sure. It's a man this time."

"Is there a but?"

"He used a knife again. Sounds like he surprised the guy." Jim was heading for the shower. When he stepped out, Marianne was waiting with a fresh cup of coffee. "You're going to need this," she said.

Jim sipped at the coffee as he stepped into the closet, his mind racing ahead. He came out of his closet wearing a pinstriped suit, with a white shirt and yellow tie, his gun clipped on. He bent to kiss Marianne, then said, "oh crap." Jim raced down the stairs and picked his folder off the counter, then rushed back up to meet Marianne at the top of the stairs.

"I need to show you a picture. Clear your mind, and when I show it to you, say the first thing that comes to mind."

"OK, go ahead."

Jim pulled the bulletin out and held it in front of Marianne.

"Oh shit. That's Bob."

Jim raised an eyebrow.

"Bob Lee. I told you about him. He was one of my roadies. A wizard with the sound equipment and lights. My last tour, we played a concert in Memphis. When we were done, he said he needed to see someone, and flat disappeared. He never came back to the bus."

"Was there a disagreement about something?"

"Not that I'm aware. He just walked away. Hank called him, but Bob's phone was off."

"Where does Bob live?"

"I don't know?"

"Do you keep employment records?"

"Jim, I've known him for years. He was a friend of the family back home. He called one day, looking for work. He was good, but he insisted we pay him in cash."

"Does he have any family?"

"No one. He's all alone in this world. I don't think it was always that way, but I'm pretty sure he's on speed."

"Really? Why?"

"I never saw him tired. You'd call and he'd be up. He was always the last one to leave, and he worked his ass off. He's skinny, and he looks older, but he's maybe sixty four or five."

"Honey, you take your gun everywhere. If you even think you see him, call 911 or call me. We are pretty certain he's our serial killer."

"I'm fine. As bad as that is, it makes sense."

"Why?"

"When I split from Brian, he was the only one that was upset by it."

"When I get home, we will talk about that. Keep your gun close and your phone on. Don't leave here unless someone is with you."

"Jim, I'll be fine. If I go anywhere it'll be with Jane."

"Do you still have his number?"

"Let me check."

Marianne picked up her phone and scrolled through her contacts. She read it off to him and he made a note of it.

Jim left after making sure that Marianne knew where her gun was, and made her promise to have it close. Then he headed to the car and roared out of the garage. He hit the lights and siren as he came up to the highway, and floored it across the bridge. On the way, he used the cars blue tooth to call Lloyd. He gave Lloyd Bob's name and age, along with the cellphone number and said he'd have more later. His next call was to Daniels. The phone went straight to voice mail so Jim left a message and rang off. Then he focused on the drive.

It was a quick run up I-5 and then crossing over on NE 50th and then a couple blocks up north on Keystone. The street was blocked by police and fire vehicles. A medic unit was sitting at the curb, idling, the medics inside sitting idle and looking bored. Lloyd and Ross stood in the doorway, watching a CSI technician at work. Sergeant Worthy stood on the porch.

"It's a wonder they can get anything," said Ross.

"Patrol was all over this place," said Lloyd. "They had to clear the house. There was a canine unit came out, and tried to track, but I don't know that he had anything."

Ross said, "I don't know. He looked like he had something."

"Probably a cat," said Lloyd.

"What do we have inside," asked Jim.

"It's a mess. She woke up and saw her boyfriend fighting with someone," said Lloyd, "the suspect swung around and stuck a knife in the boyfriends throat. She grabbed a revolver from the nightstand and got off one shot. She's pretty sure she hit him, but he took off as she fired a second round."

"Where are the rounds?"

"One went through the door and buried itself in the wall. Tech's are gonna have to dig it out.The other one went through the front door and we can't find it."

"How is she?"

"Pretty shook up. Her boyfriends dead."

"What makes you think it's our guy?"

"Look at this," said Worthy. He led them into the house on a narrow path. The front door opened into a living-dining area, with a kitchen on the left. Sitting in a chair in the kitchen was a pretty blond coed. A female officer with a dark pony tail was sitting with her. Straight back

87

was a short hallway. A spare bedroom was to the left, along with a bathroom. The main bedroom, along with it's own bathroom, was in a straight line from the front door. The body of a man, clad only in boxer shorts lay on it's back, a knife sticking out of his throat.

"The blade is the same as the others."

"This looks like a fight," said Jim.

"The girl thinks her boyfriend got up to use the bathroom and surprised this guy. She woke up to the commotion, saw them fighting and got her gun."

Jim nodded. "He looks familiar."

"He's a redshirt over at the University of Washington. He was projected as the starting running back next season."

"I still wouldn't bet against them. But maybe watch the spread." Jim knelt to look at the body. He was a well muscled nineteen, maybe twenty. He looked healthy and ready to explode for a hundred yards a game. Except for the knife sticking out of his neck.

"Where's the dog handler," asked Jim.

Lloyd pointed at a car parked across the street. An officer was in the front seat, typing on his computer. A German Shepherd sat in the back, watching intently. Lloyd crossed to the car as the dog started barking at him. The handler looked up, saw Jim, and yelled at the dog to "quiet." The dog immediately stopped barking.

"Can you show me the track," Lloyd asked as the handler buzzed the window down.

The handler got out of the car. Jim saw his name tag said "Richards." Jim waved for Lloyd and Ross to join him.

"I started out just doing an area search around the front porch," Richards began, "He picked up some tracks going into the house, which could have been the suspect or maybe cops."

"How many officers were here when you got here?"

"A lot. Anyway, we worked around the front of the house and when he got to the end of the porch he took off. I was working him on lead, and he just started pulling me along. He cut through here," Richards indicated a path that ran between a couple of rose bushes, "and ran through this yard." Richards took them on an angle across the neighbors lawn. "He ran across the street here to there," he pointed across the street, and followed his hand, then went around the corner. "The dog stopped right about here."

"Did you push him any farther?"

"I tried, he didn't want to go."

Jim pulled out his flashlight and started looking around. Lloyd borrowed the officers light. Ross stepped back. Jim and Lloyd started working the area in a circle, pushing out from where the handler said the dog had stopped.

"Hey, look at this." Lloyd indicated a damp spot in the street near the curb. Ross put on a pair of latex gloves and touched the edge of the spot.

"Engine oil," he said.

Jim stepped up on the curb alongside the spot. He looked at the curb about five feet away.

"What's this?"

Lloyd said, "looks like blood."

"OK. Have a couple officers come over here and secure this. We'll need swabs from the blood, probably from the engine oil too."

The handler spoke into his radio, and a moment later two cars came around the corner. Jim, Lloyd and Ross did a slow stroll back to the house, looking for anything that could be helpful.

"How do you know that was a good track," asked Lloyd.

"That handler trusts his dog," Jim responded.

Back at the house, Jim spoke to Sgt. Worthy. "Mike, I think we'll need a task force on this. I want you to run it."

"Understood."

"I want you to reach out to Bellevue too. What was that detectives name?"

"Marion," said Lloyd.

Right, Detective Marion. Let's set up a meeting in our office for eight AM."

"Lieutenant," said Worthy, "can I speak to you for a minute?"

They stepped off to the side. Worthy said quietly, "don't you need the captains approval to initiate a task force?"

"I called him on the way over. Mike, I hate the idea of a task force, but it needs to happen. We have a name on this guy. It's more of a fugitive task force than anything else. We just need to find him."

"Yessir."

Mike reached for his phone to call Bellevue.

"El Tee," said Lloyd, "we'll need Marianne to give a statement about our suspect."

"OK. I'll bring her in on Monday."

"Lieutenant..."

"Lloyd, you have the information. We're going away for the weekend. Unless we get really lucky today you won't need her statement for a while." He paused for a moment. "We will formalize it on Monday."

"That will be fine sir."

"Who's doing the canvas?"

"Jason and Fred. They got here right after patrol."

"OK, we're all standing around. See what they've covered, and see if you can help."

Lloyd and Ross met up with Jason on the corner. Jason had talked to an older woman on the next street. She'd seen a brown or bronze van leaving the area at about the right time, going north. She didn't know the make because she didn't know much about cars, and Jason felt lucky that she knew it was a van. When Jason told Jim, he said, "wait a minute." Then he pulled the bulletin out of his folder. In the background was the battered front end of an old Dodge van.

"Well shit," said Jim.

At eight AM sharp, Jim strode up to the podium in the basement conference room at headquarters. Flanking him was Captain Daniels, who moments earlier had found out he had approved the task force, along with Lloyd Murray and Ross Nolan and Sgt. Worthy. On the board behind him were pictures of Abigail Dunbar, Theresa May, the victim from Bellevue, and Lisa Ann Vansickle, along with her boyfriend, Jefferson Washington.

Seated in the audience were most of the homicide detectives, the Crime Scene investigators, the Chief of Patrol, the Chief of Detectives, along with a handful of narcotics detectives. Two Bellevue detectives, Francis Marlon and his partner, Julie Ann Macready, along with their Captain, Herbert Blackwell, were seated in front.

"Good morning everyone. For those of you who don't know me, I am Lieutenant Jim Churchill from SPD Homicide." He proceeded to introduce the others on stage, before continuing. "I'm going to dive right into it, and if I miss anything someone feel free to step in." There were nods from the crowd. "We are dealing with a killer who is fixated on women. He goes after them in their homes, when he believes they are alone. His first victim, Abigail Dunbar, was here on a business trip at the Olympus Hotel. She was murdered because he mistook her for this woman." Jim clicked a button on the remote in his hand, and a picture of Cassidy Upton showed up on the screen as the projector whirred to life. "Theresa May was killed, we believe, because she was involved in an accident with our suspect." Jim clicked the button again, and the picture

90

from the troopers dash cam came on the screen. "We are not sure why he went after Lisa, however he was interrupted by Jefferson Washington, Lisa's boyfriend. He stabbed Jefferson in the neck, but Lisa was able to get a hold of a revolver and fired a couple rounds at him. We believe the suspect may have been wounded, but we are unsure of the severity of his injury."

Jim looked around the room, and glanced at Lloyd. He made a go ahead gesture.

"Each scene he has left the murder weapon. In each case, they are similar in design. We believe that he purchased these knives at a pawn shop." Media relations were in the room, and he did not want the press to get everything. "These are ritualized homicides, and we have every reason to believe he will strike again."

Jim clicked the remote again. Bob Lee's picture came up. "This is our suspect. Probable cause exists for Robert 'Bob' Lee. He is sixty four years old and is a native of Texas. He was last seen driving a Bronze Dodge van." Jim gave the plate. "It has front end damage and may be leaking oil. If the van is located stop it and hold for evidence." Jim looked at the crowd. "He may abandon the van and steal another car, so keep an eye out."

Detective Marlon raised his hand. "How were you able to identify him?"

Jim's voice was steady. "This is not for dissemination to the public. He worked for Marianne Wilson as what they call a 'roadie.' He is skilled as an electrician and sound technician. Do not let his age fool you, he is quite capable. About six months ago, while she was on tour, he disappeared. Mr. Lee has a pretty serious drug habit, and it is believed that he relapsed and may be using methamphetamine."

"How did we make the connection to Ms Wilson?" This came from Ted Csysinski, the Media Relations supervisor.

"I'm sorry Ted, we cannot discuss that at this time."

Ted opened his mouth, but changed his mind after he saw the look in Jim's eye.

"Lastly, we have no idea where Mr. Lee is going. We need to find him before he strikes again."

The Chief of Detectives stood. "Jim, have you gone statewide with this?"

"We have talked to the state Attorney Generals office. We are using them to go nationwide with a bulletin. There is reason to believe that he may have ties in Texas as well as Tennessee."

"Thanks' Jim. Do we know what set him off?"

91

"We have reliable information that he believes he is doing the will of God. We think that each of these women were targeted because he believed they were committing sins against Him."

There were no other questions. "For you narcotics guys, hit up your informants. This guy has to get his meth from somewhere. For the rest of you, remember he might be switching cars. I was told he can fix and drive anything. Do not confront him alone, make sure you take back up if you find him. I'd like to see the Bellevue guys up front."

The group filed out, the two Bellevue detectives working their way up to the podium.

"Thanks for coming guys. Did I miss anything?" They shook their heads, so Jim went on. "This is Sergeant Worthy. He's in charge of the task force. Everything goes through him."

"Got it. I'd love to know how you tied him to Ms Wilson."

"I'm sure you would," said Jim.

Lloyd stepped up and said, "I've got to say something, Jim."

Jim made a beckoning motion with his hand.

"Jim, I've got to tell Bellevue."

Marlon and Macready looked at each other than said simultaneously, "tell us what?"

Lloyd looked at Jim and then said to the two detectives, "Robert Lee is targeting these women because he thinks they resemble Marianne Wilson. And before you say it, Cassidy Upton is a Nom de guerre for Marianne Wilson."

"Ohhkkaay." Julie was skeptical.

Lloyd said, "I've met with Marianne. She's currently in town visiting friends and Lee tracked her here. He was upset that she split from her ex husband. Now he's killing her a little at a time by going after women that resemble her."

Marlon nodded and said, "what's his connection with her?"

"He was a friend of the family and later worked for her. I think he was trying to look out for her. Now this, I'm not sure. But we think he's trying to track her down and kill her."

"And we are not going to let that happen," said Jim.

Jim and Lloyd stepped away to a corner of the stage.

"I'm sorry Jim," said Lloyd, "I had to tell him."

"You're fine. It had to be done, doesn't make it any easier to hear it. And thank you."

Julie turned to Francis.

92

"They aren't telling us something."

"I think I know what it is," said Francis, "you know those books I have? I've got four books by TW Griffin. When you look at the authors page, It's him." Francis was pointing with his chin.

"Are you sure?"

Francis answered, "the picture shows him wearing a tweed jacket and a turtleneck, and it shows him from the chin down to his waistline. The watch is the same, the chin is the same, the body type is the same. I'm telling you Jim Churchill is TW Griffin."

"So he's TW Griffin. What does that mean?"

"You don't read the gossip columns do you? Marianne Wilson and TW Griffin just announced they're in a relationship."

"Well that complicates things."

Jim walked into his office an hour later. Ted Cysinski was waiting for him.

"Get out of my office Ted."

"Come on Jim. This could make the department look really good."

"Or it could give you a nice soft place to land once the chief gets wise to you and throws you out."

"Jim-"

Jim interrupted him. "That's Lieutenant Churchill to you."

"Fine. Lieutenant, I can help you."

"You will. Give the press his name and his car description and tell them to call 911 if he's seen."

"Jim-uh, Lieutenant, come on. How is Marianne Wilson involved?"

"That is not for dissemination Ted."

"Don't you know her boyfriend? What's his name, TW Griffin?"

"Ted, I know I don't have a window in my office, but if you don't stick to the script I gave you I'm going to use your head to make a window."

"Come on Jim. Give me something."

"Ted, you have all you're going to get. When it's time to give you more, I'll let you know."

"Lieutenant, you know how it is. If I don't feed the monster they will make shit up."

"Good by Ted."

Ted started to say something, then thought better of it. He walked out through the bullpen, and almost ran into Captain Daniels.

"Captain, any way you can give me more than what Jim is giving me?"

"Come back tomorrow Ted. I've got nothing for you." Ted left looking dejected.

Daniels stepped into his office, and used his phone to call Jim into his office. Jim showed up a minute later.

"How did you make the connection with Marianne Wilson?"

"I showed her the picture. She recognized him instantly."

"You're on a first name basis with a lot of celebrities."

"I know some people who know some people captain."

"Close the door,"said Daniels. When Jim had, Daniels looked at him. "I know you don't think I'm very smart, but I am your captain. If you can't trust me then I can't trust you. You're supposed to be my number two, but I'll move you out in a heartbeat if you aren't straight with me."

Jim sighed. He looked at the ceiling, then the floor. Finally he looked Captain Daniels in the eye.

"OK, sir. First, for the record I know you're smart. You aren't a homicide captain by accident. And I guess I have to trust you. I haven't told you certain things because I didn't think they were anyone else's business."

Daniels made a go ahead gesture.

"When my wife died, I was a mess. Eventually I turned to writing as a hobby. After a while, I sent a book to a publisher I met when I was injured." Daniels grunted. "She agreed to publish my book under a pseudonym. My first book was published under the name 'TW Griffin.'"

"Holy shit. I have all your books."

"Thank you. Last March, I got word that someone was interested in turning my first book into a movie. One of the things I asked for was that Marianne Wilson write the music. She agreed, if she could be involved in the planning."

"So it's a working relationship?"

"Uh, no. It's gotten to be a lot more than that."

"So you showed her the bulletin as pillow talk?"

"No. When we realized she might have been the original intended victim, I had Lloyd interview her. When we had the picture, I showed it to her. She recognized him immediately."

"I see. You can't be a part of the investigation if you are in a relationship with one of the victims."

"That's why I put Worthy in charge of the task force. I want to be included, but I'm stepping back."

"Fair enough. You will not provide any further direction. Organizing the task force was your last responsibility as it concerns this case."

"Yes sir."

Jim got up to leave.

"One more thing. Anything else comes up, you let Lloyd, Mike or me know right away."

At two in the afternoon, feeling bored and frustrated, Jim slipped into his coat and left the office. So far the task force had not turned up a thing. CSI was processing the evidence from the various scenes. Narcotics was putting pressure on their informants, but no one had anything new. Jim texted Marianne and said he was on his way home. She sent him a heart emoticon.

Jim stopped at the captains office on his way out. "Sir, I'm taking Marianne to my hunting cabin for the weekend. I can't be reached by phone there."

"OK. Have fun. Are you looking for deer?"

"Of course. We both have deer tags. Maybe we'll get lucky."

"I'm sure you will," said the captain.

Jim was halfway across the bridge when he thought, "what was he doing on 520?" He'd run into Theresa May on this same bridge. But his other kills, both before and after were in Seattle. "Why was he going across the bridge?" "Aw shit," he said out loud. He hit the speed dial on his phone. There was no answer.

Jim hung up and punched the accelerator, weaving in and out of traffic. He took the exit a little too fast, and felt the back end of the Explorer start to break free. He turned the wheel slightly to the left and brought it under control. Jim realized he was holding his breath. He got onto the main road, and headed up as fast as he dared. When he got to the guard shack, he eased to a stop. The guard opened the gate, and Jim drove through. He made the right down the hill towards the water, and pulled into his driveway. Everything looked normal. He opened the garage door and backed in. He got out, and looked around. The neighbors across the street were still on vacation. A fair number of people in this community were on vacation, or business trips most of the time. It seemed like he and the Johnston's were rarities, people that worked and lived in the area. Jim was uneasy as he went into the house.

Marianne was in the bedroom. She was wearing a flannel shirt, and her new jeans. She had a duffel bag packed and her makeup bag. Jim was already packed, and their duffels were side by side. Marianne kissed him, and with her arms around his neck said, "You've been gone all day. How was it?"

Jim told her most of it, including having to tell his captain.

"Well, you knew that would happen sooner or later."

"I'm not ashamed of it. You were right."

"So what's next?"

"We are going away for the weekend. I feel like I need to get you away from here." Jim kissed her before letting her go so he could change into a wool shirt and jeans. Marianne noticed he'd switched his gun from the Glock to a 1911. Jim picked up the duffel bags, and said, "We're only going for two nights."

Marianne looked at him sweetly. "Should I bring more?"

"I'm sure this will be plenty."

"Jim, what's wrong?"

"What do you mean?"

"You're barely talking. And you look upset.

"I had a bad feeling coming home today. Bob got into a wreck on the bridge. We believe he killed the woman he crashed into. So I got to wondering, why was he headed across the bridge? Until I got home I was afraid he'd figured out you were here and was trying to hunt you."

"That seems ominous."

"I was probably just being paranoid. I think we just need to get away for a few days."

She followed him down the stairs with the rifle cases. They loaded up the Subaru and Marianne got in. Jim went back inside and set the alarm. Then they drove out and headed for the gate.

Bob had seen him drive in. He got tangled up in the sleeping bag for a moment, but he got free, and tried to run. His leg reminded him that he had hurt it the night before. He got across the street, and slid into the back yard just in time to see the garage door coming down. He crawled back to the front of that house, and limped across the street to his sleeping bag. Bob reached into his duffel, and took out a small white tab. He slipped it under his tongue. He slipped back into the sleeping bag, figuring he had some time. It took about forty five minutes before he saw a blue Subaru drive up the street. He was driving, but she was sitting in the passenger seat. She was looking at him, and talking. As they drove past, he could see luggage in the back. "What the fuck?"

He watched them drive through the gate, knowing he was stuck. He banged his fist on the ground and felt his wound break loose. Tears of frustration were flowing from his face, and dripping into the fabric of his sleeping bag. Bob packed his gear as the meth started coursing through him. Then he dragged the bag to the rear of the yard.

"How could she," he thought. There was nothing he could do. He crawled back into his bag and pulled it over him, quivering with rage. He thought about his mission and what it meant. He would have to wait now, but He knew what he must do.

Bob lay under the bushes, quivering and crying with rage. Just as dusk was turning into dark, a battered Crown Victoria rolled down the street, with it's lights off. It was time to go. He tried to stand, but his ankle was worse. He tried to put weight on it, but fell against a tree trunk. He picked up his duffel and slung it over his shoulder. Bob hobbled to the gate and unlocked it. He waited a minute, then eased through the gate, closing it behind him. The meth was giving him some strength but he was beginning to think his leg was broken. Bob limped across the street, then hid in the shadows for a moment. He stayed as far away from the street as he could, sticking to the shadows. It was two blocks to the gas station, but it took him an hour to get there. He eased behind the station, and got to his van. There was an older Honda Accord parked behind him. Cars were on either side of the van, and a guardrail in front of him. There was no way he was getting out.

He dropped on his ass and leaned against the van in despair. Then he got an idea. He crawled to the front of the gas station. There was a mail drop in the front door that people used to drop their keys after hours. He looked around, then shrugged. He had a set of tools for getting into locked cars. As a roadie he had found that musicians were forever locking themselves out of the tour bus, or limos. One of the tools looked like a long thick wire with a hook on one end. Bob looked through the slot, and could just see the keys on the floor. He pushed the tool through the slot, pulled it back and bent it in two places, then pushed it back through. The ache in his side was getting worse, and he wiped sweat from his eyes with a greasy palm.

He passed the hook over the keys, coming up just short. He pulled it out and bent it again. This time he snagged the keys. Gently he pulled them back through the mail slot. A large silver H stood out on the fob. A note was rubber banded to the key. He pulled the rubber band off and opened the note. "Battery dead. Rich." Jim smiled. He crawled back to the car and unlocked it with the key. He pulled the door open and climbed into the drivers seat. Bob pumped the pedal and inserted the key and twisted. Nothing happened. He found the hood latch and pulled. The hood popped obediently up. He limped around to the front of the car and raised the hood. Twisting at the cables, he saw they were snug. The battery looked new. He had jumper cables but there was no way they would reach.

Bob walked all around the gas station. He could find no sign of an alarm. Satisfied, he took his screw driver and went to the front door. There was no deadbolt, just an old Kwikset lock. He slid the screwdriver into the gap between the door and the jamb and pushed. The latch slid back and he was in. Bob closed the door behind him. Between the meth and the Adrenalin Bob was almost pain free. He went straight into the garage and found a portable jump starter. He turned and saw a panel by the door, a red light on top flashing.

"Shit."

He'd been inside less then a minute. He had maybe two minutes left before the cops showed up. He went back the way he had come, closing the door behind him and carrying the machine. He hooked it to the battery and flicked it on. Climbing into the car, he turned the ignition. The motor jumped to life, and he realized the headlights were on. He turned them off, then unhooked the jump starter. He tossed it into the back seat, along with his bag. Bob opened the back of the van, and pulled another duffel out before closing the doors. He would miss the van, but he couldn't use it now.

Bob got into the car, released the brake and backed into the street. As he drove out, he passed a police car going the other way. He got onto the highway, and headed east. It was almost midnight. The sign on the door back at the gas station said it opened at nine in the morning. With stops for gas and maybe something to eat, he figured he'd be in the Siskiyous and out of sight before anyone reported the car stolen.

The first officer stopped just short of the gas station. He'd seen the Honda going the other direction, but hadn't paid any attention to it. Training called for him to wait for another unit, but hell, these were almost always false. He got out of the car and walked up the sidewalk.

He got to the front of the gas station and tried the front door. It was locked. He peered inside, Everything seemed to be fine. He walked around to the back and tried the bathroom doors. When he came back around the other side, he tried the roll up doors. The one on the right rolled up with a loud clatter.

"Goddamit," he said as he pulled his gun. Then he got on radio and advised he had an open door. His partner pulled up, and together they went inside. It took maybe ten minutes to clear the entire building. When they got outside, the second officer looked on the ground and saw a piece of paper. He picked it up. "Battery dead, Rich."

"Tim, I think someone had their car stolen." He showed his partner the scrap of paper.

"Shit. Who the hell is Rich?"

"Better call the owner. He might know."

"Hey, John, remember that bulletin that Seattle put out about the bronze Dodge with Texas plates?"

"Yeah, why?"

"Aren't those Texas plates on that van?"

"Well shit."

Chapter Fourteen
Friday evening/Saturday

"Did I tell you about the horses?"

"I don't think so, Jim," said Marianne.

"I've got two, I keep stabled at Bridal Trails. They take good care of them, and I ride them when I can."

"I've been riding since I was little. When I was in 4H, I did some barrel racing."

"I don't know that these guys would make good barrel racers, but they have their own good qualities."

"You pay them to take care of the horses?"

"Not exactly," said Jim.

She raised an eyebrow, but decided to change the subject.

"How's the investigation going?"

"I've essentially been kicked off it."

"How come?"

"The Captain asked me some very pointed questions. I told him about us, and about TW Griffin."

"What does that mean for you?"

"For now, nothing. But I've been told to leave the handling of the task force and the case to Sgt. Worthy."

"That's not fair. But on the bright side if you're off the case, maybe we can spend some more time together."

Jim smiled. "Maybe."

They drove to a ranch on the east side of Bridal Trails park. Marianne was excited to see the barn and arena, and several decent sized pastures. "This is beautiful," she said.

"I like it."

He pulled up in front of a large ranch style house. A tall, thin dark haired man came out of the house, and waved. Jim waved back. "Come on, you should meet him."

Jim and Marianne approached the house. "Hello Ron."

"Hello Jim. Who is this?"

"Ron Zyminski, this is Marianne."

Ron did a double take. He swept off his hat and said, "good evening ma'am. I didn't recognize you at first."

Marianne took off her glasses, and said in her best Texas accent, "Ron, I'm pleased to meet you." Then she extended her hand, and shook Ron's. Jim thought he might die from happiness.

"He's a big fan," Jim said unnecessarily.

"Really," said Marianne, a twinkle in her eye.

Ron finally composed himself. "I'm sorry Mr. Churchill. You're here for the horses."

"It's OK Ron. She has the same effect on me."

"Down boy," said Marianne.

"Are you taking the truck," asked Ron.

"And one of the trailers. We'll be back on Sunday."

"Miss Wilson can wait here with me, if she likes, while you fetch the truck. The missus would like to meet you too."

Marianne had a pained smile on her face. "I'd love to meet her."

Ron stepped back through the open door and hollered, "June, someone here to meet you."

Marianne shot Jim a look.

June was a broad faced woman with a pleasant smile. She said, "Hello Jim. Who's your friend?"

"June, meet Marianne Wilson."

June smiled broadly. "Nice to meet you Marianne. Come and sit on the porch, I'll get us something to drink. You boys go take care of the truck."

Marianne smiled back and said, "don't mind if I do."

Ron told Jim he'd meet him at the barn, and Jim drove the Subaru around to the back of the house, where there was a small garage. He transferred their luggage to a Ford truck, putting the rifle cases into the back seat. He pulled the truck out, and then backed the Subaru into the garage, and drove around to the barn, where Ron was waiting to hook up a horse trailer.

Marianne sat in one of the chairs on the porch, while June brought out a tray with a pitcher of lemonade. As she poured, she asked Marianne how she and Jim met.

"Through work. He asked me to help on a project."

"So are you a policeman..I mean officer?"

"No," she laughed, "I'm a singer."

"Well bless your heart. Can you sing 'Nearer my God to Thee?'"

Marianne cleared her throat, and then sang, "Nearer, my God to Thee, Nearer to Thee! E'en though it be a cross that raiseth me, Still all my song shall be, nearer, my God to Thee."

When she stopped, June looked at her. "You really can sing."

"So they tell me."

"You ever use auto tune?"

"I never cared for it."

June smiled. "I was just pulling your leg. Jim took us to your concert last summer."

"What did you think?"

"You were pretty good. Can you show me how you hit those high notes?"

Ron and Jim got the trailer hooked up and led the horses inside. They had placed a bucket of water and a bale of hay for each horse. Jim had a gelding and Ron led a mare up the ramp. They were tied loosely so that they could lower their heads, and the two men eased out of the trailer and raised the gate.

"She seems nice," said Ron.

"Marianne is pretty genuine. I hate to say I've fallen for her, but dammit, she makes me feel good."

"It's been a long time since I've seen you with a woman," said Ron, "just be careful."

Jim smiled. "I'm long past that, Ron."

Ron hopped in the passenger side of the truck, and Jim drove back to the house. When they pulled up, the women were singing Amazing Grace.

Jim raised an eyebrow. "I thought she didn't sing anymore?"

"She will on occasion. She must really like Marianne."

They got out of the truck and waited patiently until they heard, "Was blind but now I see." Both men clapped in appreciation.

Jim said, "June, you sound just like I remember."

"Honey, I've learned more about singing in the last ten minutes than I ever knew," said Marianne.

"Oh don't be silly," said June, "You have an amazing voice."

"Sweetheart, they have to get going," Ron said.

"Are you sure you can't stay for dinner?"

"Oh, no thank you June. Maybe when we come back on Sunday."

"I'm counting on it"

June and Marianne exchanged hugs, and Ron and Jim shook hands. Jim and Marianne got into the truck and eased out of the yard. Marianne rolled her window down and waved at June as they drove out.

"They were delightful!"

"Good folks. They put on that aw shucks act, and that sucks you in. But they're both pretty good with the animals, and June has a head for numbers."

"How did you meet them?"

"I came out here looking to buy a horse. Wound up buying two, and a share of the ranch."

"You own that place?"

"Only a third. They needed some cash, but didn't want to lose control of the place. I was looking for an investment. Worst case, it's a tax break. But so far they're turning a profit."

"Shrewd."

They drove what Jim considered to be the back way to a small town called Fall City.

"Feel like pub food?"

"Right now I would eat my purse."

They pulled up to a tavern. Marianne pulled her hair back into a pony tail, and slipped on a pair of large glasses.

"I'm experimenting with what you told me about disguising yourself. Failed miserably with Ron, by the way."

"Well Ron's pretty observant."

"Right."

"The exception that proves the rule."

Jim found a booth in the back, and sat where he could watch the room. Marianne sat facing him and picked up a menu. Eventually the waitress came over and took their order. Jim ordered a chicken sandwich and Marianne ordered the fish and chips and a beer. When she left, Marianne reached across the table and took Jims hand.

"Is the truck yours too?"

"It is. I keep it there and Ron uses it sometimes."

"I like it. Lots of room."

The food came, and they ate in silence. No one recognized her. When they were done, Jim paid the tab and left the tip.

"Maybe we can come back sometime and canoodle."

Marianne laughed.

It was getting late. Lloyd and Ross were going back over the file again. Lloyd picked up the accident report and was reading through it. Ross was reading the Bellevue report. Lloyd stood and stretched. When he did his eyes fell on a map of the city that was stuck to the wall.

"Wait a minute," he said to himself.

103

Ross looked up briefly and went back to reading. Lloyd was staring at the map. He picked up the report and walked to the map. His finger traced across the map. Then he turned suddenly and went back to his computer.

"Ross, we missed something," said Lloyd.

Ross looked up, his interest piqued, and asked, "What do you mean?"

"Why would Lee be driving across this bridge?"

"Getting out of town? Maybe he's feeling the heat."

"Maybe. But remember, he came back into the city for another kill."

Lloyd turned the monitor on his computer so that Ross could see the display. A picture of Marianne Wilson was showing. In the background he could see the back of someone's head that looked familiar.

"You think they were canoodling?"

"Ross, where did we interview Marianne?"

"Jims house."

"Not Jims. TW Griffin's."

"Same thing, right?"

"Ross, how did we get there?"

"We drove across the floating bridge. Holy shit, do you think he figured that out?"

"Call Jim. We should head over there."

Lloyd slipped into his coat as Ross dialed the number. "Straight to voice mail."

"Come on, lets go."

"Lloyd, what are we gonna do when we get there? He's probably already left for the weekend."

"I hope so. Let's move."

They drove up onto the highway and headed east for another twenty minutes. Just before they got to the national park, Jim took a right onto a side street. He followed that almost to the end, passing a couple of houses. Then he turned left and headed up a dirt road. The truck and trailer bumped and bounced over the ruts as Jim, keeping the speed down to keep from jostling the horses, four wheeled it. About four miles up, the road ended in a wide meadow. Off to the right was a corral and stable for four horses. On the left was a shack with a small chimney. Behind the shack was an outhouse. A stream cut through the property behind the corral. Under an overhang of the roof was a stack of firewood.

"This is quaint."

"It's Shangri La."

Jim backed the trailer up to the corral. He opened the gate and lowered the ramp. He backed the gelding down the ramp, and saw Marianne doing the same with the mare. Jim opened up a couple stalls that were next to each other and using a hose filled the troughs with water from a pump. He dumped some grain into the trough. When he came back, Marianne had used a shovel to muck out the trailer. The horses were trotting around the corral, familiarizing themselves with the area.

"You didn't have to do that."

"I couldn't let you have all the fun."

Jim smiled and raised the ramp back into position. He pulled the truck over in front of the shed. Jim dumped the duffels on the porch, and unlocked the door. Marianne carried in the rifles. There was still light from the window, but it wasn't much until Jim lit a Coleman lantern that was hanging from the ceiling. As the shadows sped back into the walls, Marianne looked around the tiny cabin. There was a potbellied stove against the wall at the back of the cabin. On the left was a sink and short counter, along with a set of cupboards. A camping stove was set on top of the counter. The sink was fed by a hand pump. To the right was the sleeping area-a double bed, supported by logs with a thick mattress on top. The place was well kept if seldom used.

"There's no electricity. I'll get the stove going." Jim went out and came back with an armful of firewood. He used the smaller branches and a bit of newspaper and got the fire started. He added a few of the bigger sticks and in a few minutes the chill was leaving the room. Jim took a large coffee pot and using the hand pump filled it with water, then set it on top of the stove, while Marianne arranged the bedding. Jim admired her backside for a moment, then took a bottle of Jim Beam out of one of the duffels and a container of popcorn. He set the tinfoil container on the franklin stove, then took two glasses out of a cupboard, rinsed them, and poured a finger of bourbon into each glass. He handed one to Marianne, apologizing for not having any ice.

"I like it neat," Marianne said, a sparkle in her eye.

She had shed her jacket and boots, and was sliding around the floor in a pair of woolen socks.

"I love this place."

"We're right up against the park. Tomorrow morning we'll take the horses and work our way up into the woods about five miles. There's a spot up there that's usually good for a buck or two."

"Well, sounds like we'll need an early start," she said. Jim was suddenly conscious that she was standing up against him.

"Uh huh," he said, his throat feeling thick.

"We should get some sleep then," she said. Then she turned and walked to the bed. Jim watched as she did a slow strip tease, her back to him. Somehow Jim was able to walk to her, and kissed her.

Bob stopped in Olympia for gas, and found a Walgreens that was still open. He managed to limp inside and bought hydrogen peroxide, Neosporin and bandages. He found a brace for his ankle that he could adjust. He bought the largest bottle of Ibuprofen he could find. On the way to the counter he added a bottle of Makers Mark. The clerk never batted an eye as he paid for his items. He dumped everything into the passenger seat, then drove around to the back of the store. Parked in a spot by itself was a Honda. Acting on impulse he parked next to it. Carefully, he surveyed the lot. He didn't see any cameras, and he appeared to be all alone. He reached into the back seat and took out a screwdriver. He put the brace on his leg, which gave him support. Then he limped to the car and quickly unscrewed the rear license plate. Then he switched it with the one on the back of his car. When he was finished, he decided not to waste time with the front plate and jumped back into his car.

He stopped once in Portland and went through the drive through of a Burger King. He stopped once more, in Eugene for gas. In Grants Pass, he hung a right and followed the highway until he took the exit for a side street that led up to the National Forest. At the end of the road, right on the border, was an abandoned cabin. He pulled the car around to the back and parked. He had been popping ibuprofen and drinking bourbon to ease the pain. He had no idea how drunk or high he was. He opened the door and went inside, collapsing on an old mattress on the floor and passed out.

Marianne woke to birds chirping. The air was cold, but Jim's body was nestled against hers. She could see the stove still held some embers from the night before, but she did not want to leave the warm bed. Jims eyes were closed. He did not look like he'd be waking up anytime soon.

Marianne got out of bed, still wearing her socks, and slid across the floor. She opened the door to the stove and placed a couple pieces of kindling on the embers, gently blowing on them. Flames picked up and spread along the wood, and she fed a larger piece into the stove. Then she closed the door, and ran back to the bed. She had crawled in, when she realized Jims eyes were open.

"You son of a bitch," she cried.

Jim smiled and shrugged.

Ross and Lloyd pulled up next to the house. Lloyd thought it had an empty feel.

"Let's check with the neighbors," Lloyd said.

They got out of the car and Lloyd looked across the street. Something felt off, but he couldn't put his finger on it. They walked up to the Johnston's front door, and Lloyd rang the doorbell. They could hear giggling from inside, and a moment later Dr. Johnston answered the door. His face was red and his eyes were bright. He stood behind the door. Lloyd showed his badge and apologized for the inconvenience.

"Have you seen Jim Churchill or Marianne Wilson?"

"Honey, when did Jim and Marianne leave?"

A voice called from the other room, "I think it was five or six. No later than six I'm sure."

"That's right," said Sheridan, "they went to his hunting cabin."

They thanked him and went back to the car.

"Something doesn't feel right," said Ross.

"You noticed that too?"

Chapter Fifteen
Saturday

Francis Marlon heard the phone ranging and thought it was a dream. He opened one eye, and looked at his alarm clock. It was almost two in the morning. He grabbed the phone and held it to his ear, grunting into the receiver.

A moment later, he was shaking Julie Macready, laying next to him. "Get dressed, we got a call out."

She sat up and shook her head. "What's up?"

"Someone found the van in Hunts Point. Seattle is sending two guys, but we're closer."

Julie was out of bed, getting dressed. "Are we riding together or separate?"

"Fuck this. We'll go together. If they haven't figured it out by now, they never will."

They were dressed and moving in three minutes. Julies cell phone went off as they were getting into the car. She answered it and said, "Francis called. We're on our way." He looked at her and she said, "I still can't bring myself to tell them."

It took less then ten minutes to get to the scene. It was a small gas station on the edge of an exclusive gated neighborhood in Hunts Point. The van the task force had been looking for was sitting in the parking lot next to the building. Two uniformed Medina officers were standing behind it, leaning against a patrol car. Ross and Lloyd were leaning against the fender of their Crown Victoria.

"How the hell did you get here so fast," Francis asked.

"We took a shortcut," said Ross.

The nearest houses were separated by large fences that were covered in ivy. Julie said to the first officer, "Did anyone call a canine unit?"

"No ma'am. Didn't think to."

"Do you think this being the homicide suspects van, you might want to see if the dog could find a track?"

"Yes ma'am." He got on his radio. The nearest canine unit was coming from Kirkland.

Sergeant Worthy arrived next, driving a Ford Explorer.

"Jason is working on the warrant. Are we trying a track," he asked.

"The dog is coming," said Julie as she shot a look at the officer.

"As soon as the warrant gets here, we should open the van."

Just then the police dog arrived. The handler, a thin, wiry guy, asked what they had. Lloyd explained it to him, and he said he'd try. He harnessed up the dog and put a long leash on him. Everyone stood back to watch him work. Lloyd privately didn't think the dog would get anywhere. The first track, the handler ended up back at the first patrol car.

"Must have tracked the officer. I'll try it again."

He took the dog back to the van, and put him in a down position by the drivers door. The dog went over to the front door of the gas station and sniffed at the doorknob. Then he went behind the garage and started down the street.

"Go with him," Francis said to one of the cops, who started jogging down the street. Francis went to his car and took a portable radio out of the trunk.

They watched the dog angle across the street and started sniffing at the fence. Suddenly the dog jumped on the fence and a gate opened.

"Shit," Lloyd and Ross said simultaneously.

"What," asked Francis.

Instead of answering, Lloyd and Ross started jogging down the street. Francis looked at Julie and shrugged, then they started jogging after them. Julie shouted at the remaining officer, "stay here and guard that van!"

The dog was going back and forth in an area underneath a hedge in the front yard. Lloyd jogged up behind the second officer.

"What do we got?"

"Dunno. This is supposed to be a secure neighborhood but that gate was unlocked. Some of the families will put a gate in their fence so they don't have to walk all the way around, but they know they shouldn't leave it like that."

The handler turned and said to the detectives, "We had a pretty good track going. But it ends here and it looks like he lay here a long time."

Lloyd stood next to the handler as he reeled in his dog. He borrowed the handlers flashlight and knelt down. Looking around, he saw a spot in the dirt that was darker than the rest. "We got blood."

Lloyd slowly stood, and looked around. Looking across the street, he saw a rhododendron with a branch hanging down. Stepping around the hedge, he walked across the street. There was dried blood on a leaf. The handler had followed him around and watched with curiosity. Lloyd straightened and could just see the corner of Churchill's house.

"Shit," he said again.

Ross called Jims cell phone, but got no answer. He left a voice mail, and then texted the phone. They took the uniformed officer and walked up to the house. Francis asked Julie what they were doing. "I have no idea," she replied.

Ross looked through a window into the garage. "The explorer is here, but there's an empty spot on this end."

A light came on next door, and Sheridan called out, "I'm calling the police!"

The officer stuck his head out, "we're already here," he called.

Lloyd called from the darkness, "Dr. Johnston, it's us, Detectives Murray and Nolan."

Sheridan stepped onto the porch, knotting his robe into place. "You're friends of Jim. You were here earlier."

"That's right."

"Have you seen anyone around that maybe looked out of place?"

"Not really, no." Then he leaned back and yelled into the house, "Jane, you seen any weirdos around?"

"Just you, my love."

Lloyd couldn't help but smile. He thanked them. Before he left he went to the front door and stuck a card under the edge.

Back at the van, Jason and Fred showed up. Jason had a search warrant in hand. The CSI van was right behind him. Jason told Ray, who came on the van, to "open it up." Ray took a thin metal flat bar from a bag and in less then ten seconds had the van unlocked.

"There's blood on the seat," he said. "The back seat too."

"You see anything in there like a piece of mail with his home address, or a map with a giant X marked on it?"

"No," said Ray, "but we just got started."

The officer called out, "Hey!"

"What?"

"The plates don't match the vehicle identification number."

"You mean the VIN? We figured that."

110

"Well the VIN shows up as stolen out of Memphis Tennessee on a green van."

Ray stepped back, and looked at the door frame. "Hell, he's right. The original color is bright green, then someone spray painted the van bronze."

"Interesting."

Lloyd and Ross walked up, a little sweaty from the run.

"Find anything?"

"I just got started," said Ray.

"Mike, we have a problem."

"We found blood in the bushes across from Jims house. I think we need to tell Bellevue."

"Shit." Mike thought it over for a minute. "OK. I'll do it, but I want you there."

Mike called over to Francis. He and Julie walked up and said, "What's up?"

"We have a problem," said Mike.

Sergeant Worthy laid it out for the two Bellevue cops. When he was done, Julie said, "How do you plan on keeping this out of the press?"

Mike looked at her and paused for a moment, before Lloyd said, "The same way you don't tell anyone that you're sleeping with Francis."

Francis face colored. Julie stared levelly at Lloyd and said, "You figured that out? In what, 30 minutes?"

"More like thirty seconds. We don't care if people want to speculate, but it's not coming from us. And right now we simply need to find Jim and Marianne."

Worthy said, "We aren't going to. Daniels told me they were going away for the weekend. Churchill has a hunting cabin somewhere in the Cascades."

Francis said, "That's a lot of territory. How do we find them?"

"We don't," said Lloyd. "We'll have to wait for them."

Ray called them over to the van. "Check this out." Ray pointed to a dagger laying next to the wall of the van. "Probably fell out of a bag." The handle was two snakes intertwined and had a six inch blade.

"The bad news is he has one left," said Lloyd.

Chapter Sixteen
Saturday afternoon

Jim was leading the way down the trail on his gelding. Marianne was moving easily in the saddle. The sun was behind them. They had enjoyed the day, preferring to sit together in a grove of trees then separately in a stand.

"It is customary," Marianne was saying, "that when one goes hunting one should come back with something."

"I got some great pictures," Jim said, holding up his camera.

"Hah. I was hoping for venison."

They came out into the clearing. They hitched the horses to the railing, before they fetched and unloaded their rifles. Marianne turned towards Jim, holding her rounds in one hand and the Henry in the other. She looked past Jim and said, "Oh my God," quietly. Jim looked up at her and then following her eyes, slowly turned to look up the trail they had just come down. A gorgeous twelve point buck was staring at them. As they watched he high stepped over to the corral. He flicked his tail at them and then abruptly turned and leapt into the woods.

"I don't believe it," said Jim.

Marianne stared at the point where the deer had gone into the woods for a long minute. Finally she turned to Jim, smiled, and shook her head.

They leaned the rifles against the building, then stripped the bridles and saddles from the horses before turning them loose in the corral. Jim filled the buckets and dumped some grain into a trough.

They headed into the cabin and propped the rifles in the corner.

Dinner would be a freeze dried beef stroganoff and sourdough rolls. Marianne made a face.

He came too with the evening sun slanting through the cabin windows. He felt hot and feverish. He pulled his shirt off, and twisted to look at the wound. The edges were an angry red. He pushed on the scab, then took the dagger and pried up the edge. Then he squeezed as much of the pus out as he could get, wiping it up with a paper towel. He took a bottle of hydrogen peroxide and poured about a third of it on the wound, watching it bubble and fizz. After a while he used some paper towel to dry it. He tore open a bandage and squeezed out some neasporin. He placed the bandage on the wound, then lay back panting. He checked his ankle. He thought it seemed ok, but it still hurt to put weight on it. He ate some jerky he'd bought and drank a little water before passing out again.

Chapter Seventeen
Sunday

After breakfast, Jim and Marianne loaded their gear into the truck. Jim backed the trailer up to the corral, and dropped the tailgate. Marianne stroked the neck of the mare as she led her into the trailer. Jim clucked at the gelding and he ambled in. Jim raised the ramp and closed the gate to the corral. Marianne had climbed into the truck and was plugging in their cell phones. The batteries had been dead on all three, but as the trucks motor warmed, the smart phones glowed to life. She looked at her phone, but saw there was still no signal.

"You'll survive," Jim said as he got in the truck.

"Sure I will," said Marianne, "and so will you. I swear that phone always rings at midnight."

"It'll be about twenty minutes before they get a signal. It's the weekend, probably nothing going on anyway."

They started down the rugged dirt road, Jim taking his time. The horses didn't seem to mind. They got to the highway at about ten, and headed for North Bend.

"I'm going to top it off," Jim announced.

"Perfect. Gas stations have coffee."

"That will rot your stomach. I'll have mine black, no sugar."

Jim pulled up to the pumps and Marianne got out and stretched, her blonde hair blowing back in the slight breeze. Jim pumped the gas as she went into the station and paid for two cups of coffee. Coming out she handed one to Jim.

"I think the clerk recognized me."

"What did he say?"

"He just kept mumbling and couldn't make eye contact."

"Naw. I do that around you."

"Stop that," she smiled, "you never quit do you?"

Jim finished pumping gas and said, "You better believe it."

As they got into the truck, Marianne said, "I can't wait to take a shower."

Jim said, "That may have to wait," as he picked up his phone. There were several voice mails and text messages, most saying call as soon as you can. Jim picked one out seemingly at random and hit the call back button.

"Good morning Captain."

"Jim, is Ms Wilson with you?"

"Right next to me. What's up?"

"First, are you safe?"

"As safe as one could be when one is drinking gas station coffee."

"Where are you?"

"North Bend. We were just pulling out of a gas station. Want to tell me what's going on?"

"We found the van. We tracked the suspect to a house across the street from TW Griffins."

Now he had Jims attention. "Did you get him?"

"No, he stole another car. He swapped plates but we haven't been able to track him after that. He does not have any credit cards, not even an ATM card."

"Marianne said that she paid him in cash. What was he doing at my house?"

"We think he figured out where you live. Now that we know you're ok, we think he might have spotted you leaving. He's hurt so he might have holed up somewhere to try to get better. I want to put you and Marianne into protective custody."

"No."

"That's not a request."

"Sir, I have a job to do. And so does Marianne. We can't live in fear of this guy."

"OK. But I want you guarded for the time being."

"No."

"Again, not really a request."

"Sir, I.."

"No more arguing. We'll meet you at your house."

"I've got to drop off the horses. It'll be a while. Plus I promised a friend we'd stop for lunch."

"Where do you take the horses?"

"The Z-Bar ranch in Bridle Trails. Sir this really is not necessary."

"I hope you're right. See you at the Z-Bar."

They pulled up to the Z-Bar about an hour later. Marianne had called Ron on Jim's cell phone to explain the situation. June was waiting on the porch with a tray of sandwiches and a pitcher of lemonade. A crown Victoria bristling with antenna was parked in the yard. Daniels got out of the passenger seat as they pulled in. Jason climbed out of the drivers side, carrying a riot gun cradled in his left arm.

"Give us a minute," said Jim. Marianne got out of the truck and climbed up to the porch, where she exchanged hugs with June. Ron jumped in the passenger side and Jim drove around to the barn.

"Who the hell are those guys," asked Ron.

"One's my boss. They're here because they think we need protecting."

"He doesn't know you very well, does he."

Jim chuckled. "Thanks for that," he said.

They took the horses into the barn. Ron said he'd take care of them. Jim dropped the trailer outside, then drove around to the garage. He brought the Subaru out and drove back to the house.

"You got enough for them," Jim asked June.

"Sure."

"Y'all want a bite?"

"They look good," said Daniels and he and Jason made their way over.

Ron walked up on the porch. "Who wants to tell me and June what's going on?"

"Sir, that's a…" started Daniels.

"Captain, with all due respect, you're here. These people are friends of mine. They ought to know what you got them in to."

Daniels thought about it for a minute. "OK, but I'm not telling them, I'm telling you, understand?"

"Yes sir."

"We have reason to believe a serial killer was outside your house on Friday night."

Daniels, with help from Jason, explained about finding the van, the dogs track and finding blood in their neighbors yard.

Jim thought it over for a bit. "OK, that explains the homicide Friday morning."

Daniels made a go ahead gesture.

"He intended to kill the girl, not because she did anything wrong, but because he needed me to leave. Actually, he needed me to come back."

"What do you mean?"

"Somehow he managed to track me to my neighborhood, but he couldn't just follow me to my house."

"Come on. How could he know where you lived?"

"Marianne and I went to The Lime in Kirkland once. An article came out the next day that we'd been spotted there, only I was identified as TW Griffin, of 'Hunts Point.' All he really had to do was hang around long enough and he'd see us coming and going. But he's on a timetable. He had to get to Marianne by Friday night. So Thursday he tries to kill Van Sickle, but gets surprised by Washington."

"There's no way he could know when that would be called in."

"Unless he stops at a pay phone and calls it in. Or he drives to Hunts Point and calls from the pay phone at the gas station."

"OK. Let's assume you're right. What sort of timetable could he be on?

Jim picked his smart phone off the table, opened it and showed the screen to Daniels.

"Friday was the last day of the full moon. We have about three, maybe three and a half weeks until the next one."

"OK. So how did he figure out which house is yours?"

"We know he can pick a lock. He opened up that gate and hid out where he could see the entry." Jim was leaning back, visualizing the layout of his neighborhood. "He stayed there all day, until I came back. He spotted the house, and maybe he figured he'd do one more murder to get me called out again, then go in after Marianne while I was gone."

"Jesus!" Marianne was pale.

Jim took her hand and held it. He looked her in the eye, and didn't say anything for a minute. Her breathing slowed and her color came back. She nodded at him.

Daniels waited until Jim was looking back at him, and said, "Why wouldn't he take both of you?"

"He might try now, although I doubt it. He gets scared anytime he thinks someone has the upper hand. I doubt he'll come back if he knows I'm there. And after he got shot, I really doubted he would be back."

"Well, just to be on the safe side, we want you to stay someplace safe for a while."

"That would be my place."

"Jim…"

"Sir, he's not coming back. At least not for about three weeks. That gives us plenty of time to find him."

Daniels leaned back in his chair. Finally he said, "Alright. I trust your judgement. But you are going to get a guard detail."

"We don't need one."

"I'm willing to compromise. A week and then I'll pull it."

"Sir, I appreciate the thought, but…"

"You won't even know they're there."

"I will. OK. Seventy two hours."

"Done."

"When do thy start?"

Daniels glanced at his watch and said, "About two o'clock yesterday morning."

Chapter Eighteen
Monday

Jim woke early Monday morning. Marianne was not in bed. He washed his face and threw on a robe before looking out his bedroom window. A black Yukon with two SWAT officers sat in the street. They were wearing Oakleys against the rising sun and were parked on the wrong side of the street, facing back towards the gate. Jim shook his head and rolled his eyes, before going downstairs.

Marianne was sitting at the counter, sipping a cup of coffee. She was wearing a short robe that showed off her legs, and a pair of fuzzy slippers.

"When did you figure out what he was up to?" Marianne was terse and direct.

"Bob?" Mostly on the drive to the ranch. When Daniels was summarizing, that was when I put it all together."

"You left me here alone. Every goddam day."

"No one could have thought he'd figure out where you were. I'm pissed I didn't think of it myself."

She waved a hand. "I'm upset, yes. Not at you. Okay, maybe a little at you. But I'm scared."

Jim got out a mug and poured coffee into it. "Me too. If something happened to you I'd blame myself. The whole time I'm telling Daniels we don't need protection, I'm hoping he doesn't give in."

She sipped her coffee. "What was that thing John Wayne said?"

"'Courage isn't the absence of fear. Courage is being scared and saddling up anyway.' At least I think it was the Duke."

"That's close enough."

"Come on. We have to get going. You still have to get Cassidy ready."

"Cassidy is staying here. I'm going. With you."

Jim fiddled with the coffee pot, so she wouldn't see his eyes water.

Marianne dressed in a simple brown peasant top and blue jeans, to which she added a pair of low heels. A single strand of pearls hung around her neck. Jim was wearing a pinstripe suit. He'd put his 1911 away, and was back to carrying his Glock.

"Do you think I should bring a lawyer?"

"It's not necessary. Lloyd would probably not care one way or the other."

"OK." She brushed her hair back and gave it a final spray. "Let's go."

Jim poured two cups of coffee, and walked them out to the Yukon. He had a quiet word with them, gave them the coffee, and returned.

Marianne was waiting. When they pulled out of the garage Marianne waved at the SWAT guys. One waved back. They stayed put. "So much for not noticing them."

"I told them they were too obvious. They said they were supposed to be a deterrent. So I told them they might as well park in the driveway while we were gone."

As they drove across the bridge Marianne asked, "what are those mountains again?"

"The Olympics."

"They really stand out on a day like today," she said.

"It's the best part of the commute."

Jim parked his car in the garage. They walked into the headquarters, and walked down the stairs to the homicide office. As they walked into the bullpen, Lloyd looked up and waved. Heads were turning as people recognized Marianne.

Lloyd stood and shook her hand, "Thanks for coming in."

"I'm happy to help," she said.

"We can use my office," said Jim and led the way. Lloyd scooped a recorder and file off his desk, and followed behind.

"I'm sorry. Those guys act like they've never seen a celebrity before."

"Don't worry about it. I'm used to it."

"We might as well get started," Lloyd said. "Sir, I don't mind you sitting in, but it's probably best if I ask the questions."

"I understand Lloyd."

"This shouldn't take long."

Lloyd went through the interview carefully. He essentially walked her through everything, how she knew Bob, that he wanted to be paid in cash, and how he disappeared in Memphis, leaving them short handed. That she didn't see him again, until Jim had shown her the picture. And that she hadn't seen him in person since Memphis. When they were done, Jim and Marianne went out into the bullpen. Jason was coming in with Alan Dunbar. Jim nudged Marianne with his elbow, and indicated Alan with his chin.

"The husband," he whispered, "Alan."

Marianne approached him. "Mr. Dunbar?"

"Yes?"

"I'm Marianne Wilson. I wanted to tell you how sorry I am."

"I know who you are, miss, and thank you."

"Do you need anything? I'd love to help if I could."

"It's really not necessary."

Marianne scribbled a number on a piece of paper, and handed it to Alan. "If there is anything I can do, call this number. They can always reach me."

Alan thanked her and shook her hand. Jason started to lead him away, but Alan went back.

"Ms Wilson?"

Marianne looked at him silently.

"I've been told what happened. Do not feel guilty. Abigail would not want that. This isn't your fault."

Marianne sobbed a thank you, then hugged Alan. After a long moment, she stepped back and said, "I'm sorry."

"Please, Abigail loved your music. She'd be honored if you would attend the funeral."

"I'd love to come," Marianne said after a moment.

Thursday, eleven AM. First Baptist church."

"Jim, can we go?"

"Of course." Jim turned to Daniels. We'll leave Wednesday. I'll be back to work on Monday."

"Sounds fine to me."

Alan chimed in. "The Air Force is flying us home on Wednesday. You could fly with us."

"What do you think, honey," Jim asked.

"I've never flown with the military before. I'm in."

The press conference was at one. Daniels told Jim, "I hope you're ready."

"What do you mean?"

"You're giving the briefing."

Jim didn't say anything. There was no time to argue.

Jim was introduced to the press corp, which consisted of about twenty people. Most of them were camera and crew for the eight or so reporters. Four were local news stations, a couple of print reporters, and two of what Jim referred to as "internet reporters." Given the latest victim, some of the reporters were from the sports radio station. Flanking Jim on the stage was Captain Daniels and his assistant chief. Behind Jim was Lloyd Murray and Ross Nolan along with Francis Marlon and Julie Macready.

"As you are aware there have been three homicides in the city and east side. All of which can be related to the same suspect. Through the diligence and hard work of these detectives behind me, the suspect has been identified as Robert 'Bob' Lee, a white male, sixty five years of age. He was last seen driving a red Honda Accord. He may have switched the plates on it by now. His current whereabouts are unknown." Behind Jim, a picture of Lee was displayed, next to a photo of a Honda Accord. "If you see this man he is to be considered dangerous and armed. Do not approach on your own, but instead call 911 immediately."

There were several questions that Jim could not answer. After the fifth time saying, "I cannot answer that at this time," he thanked them for coming, gathered up his papers and followed Daniels off the stage to his right. One of the reporters rushed up to him and said, "Lieutenant, can you answer a couple of questions for me?"

Jim looked at her icily, and said, "the press conference is over ma'am."

"Is it true that Marianne Wilson is involved in this investigation?"

"I'm curious as to where you might have heard that."

"You know I can't release my sources. So is it true?"

"I'm not at liberty to discuss any one individuals involvement with this case."

"I have it on good authority that she is not only involved in the case, but that she's in a relationship with one of the detectives."

"Good bye ma'am." There was steel in his tone.

Marianne was waiting by the elevator. "She looked right at me and didn't recognize me."

"It's the glasses."

"I think she's one of the video tabloids. She probably has a whole story ready to go. Along with "Police will not confirm the report.""

"Well, she's off our Christmas card list then."

He didn't so much as wake up as he came to. He drank water from the sink, and ate more jerky. Sooner or later he'd have to go into town and get food, but for now he had enough for a few more days. He stood at the sink and tried to plot his next move. His brain wasn't working right. Finally he went to his duffel, and found another tab. He bit down on it, and swallowed, the pill tasting bitter. As the chemical coursed through his body, his mind started working with increasing clarity.

He stripped off his shirt, and peeled the bandage back. The wound looked better, like it was healing. He changed the bandage, adding more ointment to the gauze. He went outside and looked at the car. Bright red just wouldn't do. He went to the shed, and found another case of paint. Things were starting to look up. Just a matter of time now.

Chapter Nineteen

Abigail's body had been transferred to a funeral home. Jim and Marianne met with Alan and rode with him in his rental car behind the hearse. They rode in silence until they passed through Tacoma.

"When do you think you'll find him," Alan asked.

"Should be soon. We just have to figure out where he is."

"Guy like that, you should shoot on sight."

"We aren't the Wild West out here."

"If I could I'd kill him with my bare hands. That woman was my life."

Jim looked at Marianne. "I know how you feel. But..."

"Lieutenant, I've seen the way you look at her when you think no one is watching. That's how I used to look at Abigail. Are you telling me you wouldn't kill the guy that..." He paused for a moment. "Shit, I'm sorry ma'am."

"Don't worry about it Alan. I understand what you're saying," said Marianne.

They arrived at the gates to McChord Airfield and were waved through by the gate guard. They drove directly onto the airfield to a waiting C-141 with a lowered ramp. An Air Force honor guard was waiting in their dress uniforms with white gloves. The hearse made a wide arc, then backed up and stopped about ten feet from the guard. They got out of the rental as the driver and passenger got out of the hearse. Jim, Marianne and Alan retrieved their luggage from the trunk of the car. Alan handed the keys to the car to one of the men from the hearse. Marianne had packed two suitcases and her makeup bag, which she thought would be reasonable for just five days.

A master sergeant barked out commands to the small group, and the coffin was taken out of the back of the hearse. Six men carried the coffin up the ramp in a slow procession. A detail of enlisted men appeared and picked up the luggage, carrying it onto the plane. A lieutenant approached and exchanged salutes with Alan. Jim and Marianne followed Alan up the ramp. Marianne realized that the seats all faced the rear of the air craft. The honor guard was standing by the coffin. Alan nodded at the master sergeant, who issued a "fall out" command. The guard relaxed as Alan shook hands with each of the enlisted men, thanking them. The ramp started going up, and everyone took their seats. Jim and Marianne sat behind Alan, as he sat in the last/first row, facing the coffin.

"Why are the seats backwards," asked Marianne.

"Some people think it's safer if the plane crashes," answered Jim.

"I wish I hadn't asked."

The plane taxied out onto the runway and paused a moment before revving up the engines. The pilot released the brakes and the plane gathered speed, taking off without a hitch. The plane reached altitude and settled into a cruise. Alan remained at his seat. Jim stood and stretched in the cramped space. A young lieutenant in a flight suit appeared, and said, "Colonel Dunbar?"

Jim pointed at Alan.

"Sir, with the pilots compliments, he'd be honored if you'd join him in the cockpit."

Alan nodded and stood, then went forward.

Marianne unbuckled finally, and stood. A couple of the honor guard were staring in her direction. She noticed but didn't say anything.

"You know what would make their day?"

"What's that?"

"If you went over and talked to those guys. Maybe sign something for them."

"Are you sure? I wouldn't want to violate some sort of protocol."

"It's ok. Just go say hello."

"You come too."

She took his hand and led him over. As they approached, the two young men, not knowing what else to do, jumped to their feet.

"Hello boys," she said.

One of them managed to stammer out "ma'am."

"How old are you two?"

"Nineteen ma'am," they both said.

"Where y'all from?"

"Texas ma'am."

"Arkansas ma'am."

Jim could feel her relax as she spoke to the two airmen. Soon the other members of the Honor Guard approached, and they were all talking and laughing. The master sergeant came up behind Jim.

"She just made these boy's day."

"I bet she did."

"I'm Master Sergeant Darryl Bonham."

"Jim Churchill." They shook hands.

"I knew a James Churchill once. Gulf War two. I was a forward observer attached to an army company."

"Must have been a while ago."

"Not that long. You still look the same Captain."

Marianne was learning how to sing a cadence from one of the honor guards.

"You too, Darryl. Still going out in the field?"

"Only if they pitch a tent in my hotel room."

They arrived at Arnold Air Force base about four in the afternoon. Darryl and Jim had caught up, then Marianne came back. Alan returned from the cockpit about half way through the flight. Marianne took Jims hand as the plane touched down and rolled to a stop on the tarmac.

A hearse was waiting for them as the ramp lowered, and Abigail's coffin was brought out. She was placed gently into the hearse, then Alan, Marianne and Jim got into the back of the waiting limousine. As they small caravan rolled out Alan opened a panel in the back, revealing a mini bar. He offered drinks to Marianne and Jim, which they gratefully accepted.

"I heard that Master Sergeant call you Captain."

Jim swirled the brownish liquid in his glass. "He did."

"Were you Air Force?"

"Army. He was assigned to my unit as an FO."

"Iraq?"

"Yes sir."

Alan sipped his drink. "That's where I met Abigail."

He slipped into silence again. Marianne leaned against Jims shoulder and fell asleep. Jim sat quietly, not wanting to disturb either of them.

The funeral home had stayed open late to receive them. Alan had the limousine take Jim and Marianne to their hotel. On the way, Marianne told Jim about her house outside of Nashville. He agreed they should drive there after the funeral. They got out at the Crowne Plaza. The valet helped with the luggage and they approached the counter.

"I need to arrange a car I can drop at the airport in Nashville," Jim said.

"No problem sir. I'll have one delivered."

They went up to their room. They took in the view and looked around the spacious suite. Marianne found the mini bar, and poured them both some drinks. Jim felt rumpled in his suit, and peeled off the jacket. Marianne handed him a glass, and they toasted their good health.

"God, I feel so sorry for him," said Marianne.

"I know. He hardly talked."

"How do you know what to do in those situations?"

"When my wife died, I really resented people trying to push me to open up. I was angry and sad and frustrated that I couldn't do more. I imagine he feels the same way."

"Please explain? It doesn't seem like there were any problems in their marriage."

"There's problems in every marriage. Maybe she was stressed because of the situation with her old boss. Maybe he was upset that she was spending too many hours at work. I don't know. But anytime in something like this there's a feeling of guilt on the part of the survivor."

"How did you get past it?"

"I drank a bit. I'd wake up in the morning with a hangover and I'd still be pissed. I was mad that I didn't do more, but I'd done everything I could. It took me a while to realize that."

"How long?"

"After three or four years, I found I could date. I'd go out with a woman once and I'd find some flaw in her that I couldn't stand so there wouldn't be a second date. Did that maybe a half dozen times. Finally I stopped trying all together."

"What was different with me?"

Jim smiled. "The truth?"

"Please."

She was wearing a black knee length dress with long sleeves. She stood with her arms crossed, her drink in one hand and her right foot forward.

"I saw you on TV. I was impressed with how intelligent and witty you were in that moment. That was about the time I was getting offers to turn my book into a movie. So I purchased a couple of your albums. Then the other two. Started watching your videos on YouTube and thought you had something special. So I asked that you be approached about writing the theme song."

"You were stalking me?" She had a twinkle in her eye.

"Maybe a little. But in my defense, I did not expect to connect with you."

"In your defense, maybe I read your book and wanted to meet you."

He took her drink and set it on the table, then pulled her to him and kissed her. She kissed back, then put a hand on his lips and said, "I'm going to faint from hunger if I don't eat something soon. There's a dining room in this hotel, it should still be open."

"Yes ma'am. Room service?"

Putting on a mock British accent, she said, "That would be divine."

Thursday morning

Jim awoke to the sun streaming through the window. Marianne was already putting on makeup.

"How long have you been up?"

"About an hour. You forget we're on my turf."

Jim nodded, and went into the shower. In 3 minutes he was showered and shaved. He had a black Armani suit with a white shirt that he slid into. As he was knotting his tie, the room phone rang.

"Sir, the man from the rental agency is here with your car."

"We'll be right down."

Marianne had on a high necked long sleeved dress with black hose and low heels. Jim knotted his tie and they made their way to reception. They met the agent for the rental.

"I'm sorry sir, the only thing we had left was a new Dodge Charger."

"I guess that will have to do."

He did the walk around. A black Daytona with a navigation system and leather seats. He signed for the car, and they took the elevator back to their room. On the ride up, Marianne said, "I think I'm gonna like that car."

When the service ended, they drove in the procession to the cemetery. The honor guard was there, three of them forming a rifle team with M-14 rifles. When the service ended, they raised their rifles and fired three times, in unison. Once the casket was lowered into the ground, Alan sought them out and asked them to come to the wake. They agreed, and said they couldn't stay long.

In the car, Marianne said, "he seems attached to you."

"To us really. We represent something to him. Maybe a connection he perceives to his wife."

They found his house, and parked the car in the driveway. A valet took the keys, and gave them a ticket. The two of them found their way inside the house. On the walls Jim noticed photographs of Alan and Abigail, playing tennis, fishing, golfing. They seemed to lead an active lifestyle. Marianne saw a buffet table and steered them to it. It was almost four in the afternoon, and they'd had little to eat besides coffee. They filled a plate, and sat at a table with some of the other guests. They all seemed to know each other, and it was a while before they realized who Marianne was.

They chatted amiably with some of Knoxvilles more elite, then Jim made his way to Alan. Standing just off to the side was a tall blond woman. Alan whispered in her ear, and she left. They shook hands with Alan, and he pulled Jim in close. "I don't care what it takes. You find him you kill him."

"I can't guarantee that," Jim whispered back. "It's best you know that up front. I won't kill him unless I absolutely have too. I will not commit murder."

"Jim," Alan said, "you have to know if this goes to trial they are going to crucify you."

Jim raised an eyebrow.

Alan went on, "you and Ms Wilson are in a relationship. The defense is going to say your judgement was colored."

"Doesn't matter," Jim said, "I won't commit murder."

"I knew you'd say that," Alan said. "You're a good man. Don't let anyone ever get to you."

Jim and Marianne left Alan Dunbar in the house, talking to the blond woman that Jim was quietly referring to as 'Frosty.' They found the valet, who fetched the car, and Jim found his way to I-40.

"Keep your eyes on the road, mister," Marianne said. She undid her seat belt and leaned the seat back, then slid into the back seat behind Jim. He couldn't help but watch in the mirror as she slid out of her dress and panty hose, sliding on a favorite pair of torn jeans. She took her slip off over her head, and looked into the mirror, meeting Jims eyes.

"Pervert," she said. Jim smiled.

She put on a t shirt, and sneakers, then reversed the trip, ending up back in the front seat. Jim had loosened his tie.

"That was slick," he said.

"You peeked."

"More like gawked."

"Can I ask a serious question?"

"How much trouble am I in," Jim asked.

"I mean it. I want to be serious for a minute."

Jim took a deep breath, then said, "ok."

"What's going to happen to Alan?"

Jim visibly relaxed. "What do you mean?"

"I was doing some thinking. Abigail and Alan seemed pretty tight. And now she's dead. It must feel like he's lost a limb."

Jim thought for a minute. "Yeah, that'd be about right. Obviously I didn't have that great a marriage before my wife died. But there was a deep sense of loss, and a feeling like I should have done something different. But I think he'll be fine."

"What do you mean?"

"Did you see his secretary?"

"Are you trying to make me jealous?"

Jim smiled, "no honey. I only have eyes for you. But did you see how she looked at him?"

"Not really," Marianne said, "why?"

"His secretary is in love with him. Probably has been for a while. Once he's past the grief stage, I hope he figures that out."

"You don't think…?"

"I doubt it. I have a feeling that Alan is a very contained man. I doubt he ever did anything adverse to his marriage."

"But?"

"I just hope we get to Bob Lee first."

At the first rest stop, Jim asked if she wanted to drive. Jim shed his tie and they switched seats before Marianne took them into Nashville, driving much faster than Jim was comfortable with. Marianne's ranch was just west of the city. She turned into her driveway a little after six, pulling up in front of a large house. The exterior was peeled logs. A woman came out of the front door, and smiled when she saw Marianne. She was introduced as 'Rosa', the cook and housekeeper. Jim gathered her husband also worked on the ranch, taking care of the animals.

Jim brought in their luggage, and Marianne took him to the bedroom. He dumped the luggage, and looked around. The room was neat, if a bit cluttered. The bed was covered in decorative pillows, but was large and looked comfortable.

"I'm a bit overdressed," he said.

"You look fine. Come on, I'll show you around."

Jim lost count of the bedrooms. She took him into the basement. "This is my office," she said. At the back of the basement was a small recording studio. The walls were lined with guitars. A drum set and keyboard were pushed up against a wall. Amplifiers of various sizes lay against another wall. A wet bar with a refrigerator took up space along the wall as well.

"Some of my friends are coming by later," Marianne said, "I've been gone a while and we need a session."

"Mind if I watch?"

"Not at all. Some of them are kind of free spirits."

"Cool."

About an hour later people started showing up. Her drummer, the bassist and a guitar player. A woman in her forties showed up, and introduced herself as Jenny, the backup singer. Jim was the only one in a suit, although he had shed the tie. Marianne introduced him, then he took a seat on a bar stool to watch them work. Marianne took them through some warm ups, and then launched into "Storms Never Last" to get things started. Jim leaned back against the bar, with a feeling he was watching a professional at work.

When they finished the entire group did a self critique. Jim thought it seemed similar to tactical debriefings that he had been involved in. Once they felt they had it right, they moved on to the next song, and repeated the process. Jim noticed that as a group, they were perfectionists.

After about an hour, they took a break. Marianne was talking something over with her backup singer. The bassist and the guitar player were talking animatedly as they walked towards the bar. The guitar player got two beers from the refrigerator and handed one to the bassist. He returned to the stage. The bassist approached Jim and shook his hand.

"Ted, right?"

"Yep, Ted Bruski."

"Did you play for the Patriots?"

Ted laughed, "Nope. That's Bruschi. I'm Bruski, like ski."

Jim smiled. "Got it. How many times you hear that?"

"Too many. So, are you a cop?"

"Interesting segue. A long way from here maybe. Why?"

"You're carrying a gun. Marianne introduced you as her boyfriend. I figured you're not a body guard."

"Maybe you ought to be a cop."

"Thought about it once. Somebody thought I had a talent, so I'm here now."

"Funny how life works, isn't it?"

"Yeah it is," said Ted. "So is it true about Bob?"

"Most of it. How well do you know him?"

"About as well as anyone. We were all part of a big family." Ted leaned in close, "Don't tell Marianne, but he was pretty heavy into meth."

"What do you think happened to him?"

"I think the drugs short circuited his brain."

"You have any idea where he might be?"

"He told me once he had a place in Oregon."

"Lot of territory. There's no record of him owning a place."

"He told me he had found an abandoned house he squatted in. Like southern Oregon."

"OK."

"Let me think. He mentioned Medford once, but that's not it."

Jim pulled out his cell phone and opened a maps app. He typed in Medford Oregon, and showed it to Ted.

"That's it. Grants Pass."

"Hey, that's great. Thanks man."

They chatted some more, than Marianne called them back to the stage. Jim looked at Marianne and held up his phone. She nodded and he stepped out of the room.

He had to go upstairs to get a signal. When he did, he dialed up Lloyd's number.

"What's up, Lieutenant? You still in Tennessee?"

"As a matter of fact, I am. I just spoke to Marianne's bass player. He told me that he remembers Bob Lee squatting in a place near Grants Pass."

"That's interesting. I'll call the PD down there."

"I'd call the county too. What is that, Josephine county I think."

"Yeah, they can start trolling some of those back roads. Hey, I think you might be right, there's been nothing since the end of the full moon."

"Marianne is worried. I think she's thinking about staying here. But he knows this place, too."

"Jim, I know you're worried about her, but she's pretty capable."

"So was Abigail Dunbar."

When Jim came back, he slid in, quietly closing the door behind him. Marianne had a guitar and they were working their way through a tune he wasn't familiar with. They stayed at it for another hour, until Marianne said, "ok guys. Not bad for the first time in a while."

As if by magic, Rosa appeared, carrying a tray loaded with sandwiches. She set them on the bar and just as quickly disappeared. The band gathered around, loading sandwiches on plates. Ted said to Jim, "you better hurry before they're all gone."

Jim got a plate and plucked a sandwich at random from the dwindling pile. Beer was being passed around. Jim talked to everyone there, although no one volunteered anything new about Bob Lee. Jim was watching Marianne. They had been rehearsing for a couple of hours, but her eyes shone, and she still projected energy. When the food was gone, Marianne announced, "I'm going back to Seattle on Sunday. I'll be back soon, and we'll do this again. We all have stuff to work on, so stay with it. I love you guys."

Hugs and handshakes were exchanged, and one by one the band filed out. When they were gone and they were alone, Jim asked, "are you sure you want to come back with me?"

Marianne said, "don't you want me to?"

"Of course I do. But I'm worried about your safety."

"I know you'll keep me safe. What am I going to do, stay here? This is no guarantee either. He's been here, Jim."

Jim considered that. "OK. But you carry your gun. Not in your purse. On your belt. And everywhere."

"Alright. But only if I can get matching holsters."

"I'll buy you a black one. Black goes with everything."

Chapter Twenty
Friday

Jim opened his eyes. Marianne was laying with her head and chest on him, and her right leg draped over him. He looked at the clock by the bed and saw it was seven. It took a moment for him to realize he was waking up to Seattle time in Nashville. Jim watched her breath, not wanting to disturb her peace.

Finally, she opened her eyes. Without moving, she looked at him for a moment.

"Isn't this where we left off?"

"I think so," Jim replied.

She kissed him, then reluctantly rolled off him. Jim stood up, and asked, "do I need a robe?"

"Rosa and Miguel live on the ground floor. Maybe put some pants on."

"I hope you didn't keep them awake."

Marianne threw her pillow at him, then took his pillow, and laid back down.

Jim found a pair of jeans and slipped them on, then a t shirt and made his way to the kitchen on the ground floor. Rosa was in the kitchen, a robe and nightgown covering her stocky build. Miguel sat at the table, a red and black flannel shirt with the sleeves rolled up over thick forearms.

"Good morning," Jim said as he poured two cups of coffee.

"Mister Jim," said Rosa, "Miguel would like a word with you."

"Please, just call me Jim. What's up?"

"Mr. Jim," said Miguel, "Marianne is like family to us." Jim nodded, so Miguel went on, "she has been very good to us over the years. She got married, and we did not care for him, but she thought it was love and married him anyway."

133

"She told me a little about that." Jim took a seat at the table, across from Miguel.

"Anyway, she left him. I no care what he said in the magazines, she had enough and left." Jim made a go ahead gesture.

"Her heart was broken. She drink too much for a few days, then she tell Rosa she was done with men."

Jim was hoping he would get to the point. The coffee was cooling off.

"She get call from Hank. He say go to Seattle. Meet Mr. Griffin. Maybe do a movie. You feel better."

Jim sipped his coffee.

"Almost a month later she come home with you. Now she say you the love of her life."

Jim choked on his coffee, then recovered. "She said that?"

"Yes, mister Jim. Maybe not in so many words. But yes. So I tell Rosa, what he doing? He after her money?"

"Miguel, I…"

"You listen, Mr. Jim," Miguel interrupted, "I not finish yet. This girl, she like a sister to me. I see you taking advantage of her, I see red. Rosa, she say talk to him first. So I tell you this, Mr. Jim. You hurt her, you have to deal with me."

"Can I talk now?"

"Yes, Mr. Jim."

"Miguel, did she tell you who I am?"

"She say you hot shot detective."

"Big shot, Miguel," said Rosa.

"I do that too, although I wouldn't call me a big shot. Miguel, I didn't intend to fall for Marianne, and I don't think she meant to fall for me. But we did. The last thing in the world I want is for something to happen to her."

"I hope not, Mr. Jim."

"Miguel, fear not. I'll do everything in my power to protect her."

"You better."

"Miguel." Jim leaned in close, almost whispering. "I would rather die than see Marianne hurt. But if you do decide to come after me, pack a lunch."

Jim stood, and picked up the coffee. He dumped out Mariannes, and poured fresh into the cup before heading upstairs.

Marianne was sitting at her make up table, wearing a long robe, brushing her hair. "What took so long?"

134

Jim looked down the hall for a moment, then closed the door. "I had to explain to Miguel that your virtue is safe with me."

She laughed, "stop it."

Jim set her coffee down, and peeled off his shirt. "I'm stepping into the shower."

"Not yet, I want you to protect my virtue," she said, as she stood and grabbed at the belt on his jeans.

"It's not your virtue I'm worried about," Jim said.

It was almost an hour before Jim and Marianne untangled and took showers. They dressed and went downstairs. Rosa was still there.

"Mr. Jim, I must apologize for my husband."

"Don't worry about it Rosa."

"He is too protective sometimes."

"I understand." To Marianne he said, "He was pretty forceful."

They ate eggs and bacon, and drank more coffee. Marianne asked if he wanted to ride a horse. They went to the barn and saddled up, and cantered towards the park.

The clock showed two hours later in Seattle. Lloyd was typing up notes to another case when his phone rang.

"Detective Murray."

"Deputy Stiina, Josephine county. We have a couple of houses could be possibles."

"Cool. Do you have pictures?"

"We do, plus some video from a helicopter."

"Can you email them to me?"

"They're on the way."

They exchanged small talk while Lloyd opened his email. There were three files attached.

"Which one is the most remote?"

"The first one I sent," Deputy Stiina said.

Lloyd opened the file. The house seemed to be in decent shape and there were a number of outbuildings that would be useful. What caught Lloyds attention was tire tracks in the yard. It looked like a car had pulled right up to the back door, and then into a barn. He looked at the other two, but none had the tracks.

"Can you get close surveillance on that first one? I think that's a real possibility."

"For how long?"

"Couple days maybe. If he doesn't show by Monday, maybe check the house."

"If we see anything, we'll call you. If he's squatting there we might need a warrant."

"If he's not back by Monday he won't be back. Then the place would be abandoned and you won't need a warrant."

"I'll talk to my boss. We're a pretty small department."

"Call me back, either way."

Twenty minutes later the phone rang again. "Deputy Stiina again, detective. My lieutenant says we don't have the manpower for a stakeout for this. His actual words were something like not on a hunch, he will never get a search warrant for this. How do you feel about us doing a knock and talk?"

Lloyd thought it over for a minute, shrugged and said, "I'm okay with a couple of you guys going up and knocking on the door. Just remember, he's killed three people. We know he doesn't like to be confronted, but the last guy that tried to stop him got stabbed in the neck. If you go up there, be careful."

"OK, I'll call you back when we're done. If he's there, we'll set up a perimeter and call you."

"OK. If I know for sure he's there a warrant won't be a problem."

"Copy that. We'll be careful."

Deputy Stiina and his partner, Deputy Lindahl, met at the house. It took the better part of an hour to reach it, driving carefully over rough roads. They got out of their cars at the edge of the yard. Other than the outbuildings the yard was empty. The whole place had a vacant feel to it.

"How do you want to do this?"

"I think we ought to just walk up to the front door, peek in the windows and knock on the door, " said Stiina.

"Let's do it."

They fanned out as they walked across the yard, moving evenly across the long grass, about fifteen feet apart. They got to the bottom of the stairs. Lindahl moved up first, Stiina right behind. Lindahl looked through the front window. There was some small clutter but nothing that stood out. Stiina knocked on the door, but there was no response. They moved around the porch to the right, not seeing any sign that anyone was home. They were able to peek into a kitchen and then a bathroom. In a back bedroom, they could see a mattress on the floor, and what looked like bloody bandages.

"Shit, look at this."

Lindahl had crossed past the back door, and was looking in another bedroom. The walls were papered with pictures. Marianne Wilson was on stage in some. The angles on those were from behind. There were some of her eating in a sidewalk café, probably in New York. There was one of a her in a club, with a tough looking guy with a short haircut and a designer suit. There was another woman too, with dark hair and an overbite. There was Marianne in front of a big cabin. Lindahl had taken out his smart phone and was taking pictures through the window.

"I think we have to go in," said Stiina.

"Why? What's the rush?"

"There are bloody bandages in the other bedroom. He could be bleeding out inside."

"OK," said Lindahl, and slid his phone back into the cargo pocket of his pants.

Stiina stood to the left of the door and drew his gun. Lindahl drew his. Stiina knocked on the door before trying the door knob and pushed. The door started to open, then hesitated for a moment before Stiina's momentum pushed it past whatever was holding it up. There was an audible popping noise from deep in the house, then smoke filled the air inside. Stiina and Lindahl turned and ran off the porch, trying to get distance from the house. They felt a sudden whoosh of air being pulled past them, then felt the heat on their backs as the fire pushed them off the porch. By the time they could get turned around the house was engulfed in flame.

Stiina keyed up his mic, and got a tone telling him he was out of range. They moved around the house and got back to their car. Stiina got the same tone again, so he got into his car and started it. He keyed up the microphone, and his dispatcher answered him.

"We need fire here. The house is fully involved, and it could spread to the trees. Send a sergeant, this is probably an arson."

Lindahl was staring in shock at the house.

"Hey, you ok?"

LIndahl blinked and came out of it. "Just a little singed. What the hell was that?"

"I think Seattles murder suspect booby trapped his house. I got to call them, but I'm getting no bars. How about you?"

"No bars. They'll just have to wait. Damn man, I think I shit my pants."

Jim and Marianne got back to the barn a little after four. They stripped the saddles from the horses and brushed them before putting them in their stalls with some hay and water. They walked back to the house to find Rosa serving up chili to Miguel. She pointed with her chin to a pair of bowls on the table and said, "help yourselves."

"She makes the best chili around," said Marianne.

Jim ladled some into each bowl and slid a piece of cornbread out of the pan. They sat at the table. Miguel had the television on a Spanish news station. They ate quietly, side by side. Jim was almost finished when Marianne said, "Jim look! We're on television."

Jim looked up and saw themselves coming down the steps at the front of the First Baptist Church of Knoxville. Marianne had her hat on and both of them were dressed in black, looking somber. They saw themselves speaking with Alan Dunbar as the announcer spoke rapidly in Spanish.

Miguel translated for them. "They're saying that Ms Wilson was at the funeral for Air Force major Abigail Dunbar, who also worked as an executive at Nav-Par navigation systems. They don't know what the connection is that you have with the Dunbars, but they said you flew out with the body. That while you were on the plane it is reported that you spoke with and signed autographs for the Honor Guard, and that you sang with them."

"More like they sang with me. Actually taught me one of their marching songs."

"A cadence," said Jim.

"Right, a cadence. What else did they say?"

"That's pretty much it," said Miguel. The screen changed and displayed an overhead view of a house on fire in a remote area. No one was really paying attention until Jim said, "Turn that up."

Miguel did and started to translate, but Jim held up a hand. Jim watched the television for a minute, then announced, "I need to make a phone call. I'll be right back." He left the table and went upstairs.

"I don't understand," said Miguel, "it's a house fire."

"Where is it," asked Marianne.

"Someplace in Oregon,," said Miguel.

Marianne followed Jim upstairs. She found him in the bedroom, talking into his work cell phone.

She heard him say, "Well let me know when you hear anything."

"What's going on?"

Jim looked up. "That fire is probably related to the case. Lloyd thinks that's where Lee was holed up. A couple deputies were going up there to see who was there. They haven't called back yet but the area is pretty remote so it's likely cell phones don't go through."

"Jesus. All you could see was smoke and fire. How could anyone survive that?"

Jim didn't answer.

"By the way, when did you learn Spanish?"

"I took a course in college," he said.

Bob was coming back from town when the fire truck passed him. There wasn't any doubt in his mind where they were headed. He jockey'd the car around and drove back to town. He pulled into a gas station and did a quick inventory. He had food and water and methamphetamine. More importantly, he had the last knife. He pulled up to the pumps, and topped off the tank. Then he headed towards the freeway and started heading north. As he drove he popped another tab into his mouth.

Chapter Twenty One
Friday evening

It was after five in the evening when Deputy Stiina called.

"Sorry I couldn't call earlier. Things went to shit down here."

"I heard. It's all over the news. What happened?"

Stiina filled him in. "The place is virtually destroyed. I don't see how anything survived that."

"You'd be surprised. Are you guys hurt?"

"Sunburned maybe. And I have to buy a new pair of pants."

"I don't blame you. Are you able to to investigate the scene?"

"We think the fire is pretty much out. But they're worried about reignition. They're leaving a truck here all night, just in case."

"OK. I'm going to try to get someone there as early as I can."

Lloyd hung up the phone and debated his options. He called Sergeant Worthy, who picked up on the third ring and filled him in on the Josephine County situation.

"Daniels won't approve that. He'll say just let them sort it out."

"Sarge, they won't know what they're looking at."

"Doesn't matter. He won't do it."

"Well, how about if I call him anyway." Before Worthy could answer, Lloyd hung up. Daniels answered the phone on the first ring, and thought for a long minute.

"We can't even say it's the right place."

"What else would it be?"

"I can't approve it. We'd have to be able to show it's connected and we can't."

Lloyd hung up exasperated. He thought over his options for a full five minutes. Then he made a phone call.

When Jim answered, he and Marianne were just leaving Coyote Ugly Saloon. Lloyd could hear noise in the background. He was pretty certain Marianne was listening in. Lloyd explained the problem to Jim. His response surprised him.

"I've always wanted to go to southern Oregon at this time of year. Since I'm still burning my own time, I think maybe I'll swing through Grants Pass. Can you call and tell them I'm coming?"

"Will do, and thanks Lieutenant."

Jim hung up and Marianne said, "When do you want to leave?"

"Tonight, if I could."

"Don't you mean we?"

"Aw man. This is going to be a crime scene. It could be dangerous."

"Staying here could be dangerous." Marianne was serious. Bob knew where her house was.

"Honey he may still be in the area."

"I don't care. I'm going with you," she said.

Jim pulled out his smart phone, "Fine. I'll see if I can get us on a red eye tonight."

"I've got a better idea," she said with a smile.

Marianne extracted her phone from her purse, and speed dialed a number. Hank, her agent, picked up on the other end.

"Hank, I need a favor."

"Marianne, when are you going to get back in the studio?"

"Soon Hank, I promise. We're working on some songs, and I got together with the band yesterday. Hank, you still owe me."

Hank sighed, "what do you need?"

"I need the Gulfstream."

"When do you need it?"

Marianne mouthed, "When do you need it," at Jim. Jim looked at his watch, did some quick mental calculations, then said, "Midnight."

"Midnight."

"Marianne, that's asking a lot."

"I knew you'd come through for us."

"Fine. Be at the airport by eleven. There'll be a crew waiting." He gave directions to the gate, and Marianne hung up her phone.

"We'd better get packed," she said.

"Your agent has a Gulfstream?"

"We rent one from time to time. You'll like this one."

At ten thirty they were at the airport with their bags. Jim had his customary duffel and was wearing his black Armani suit. Marianne had two suitcases plus her makeup bag. Jim wasn't sure what she packed but since he was carrying the bags he knew how heavy they were.

They made their way to the private section of the airport and were introduced to the captain and copilot. They boarded the G500 and stashed their luggage. The co pilot showed them the interior, seats and a table up front, the back section set up as a two bed bedroom.

"Feel free to rack out if you need to," said the copilot, "it's going to be about six hours before we get to Medford. We'll be stopping once in Denver. We could go straight through, but the captain is concerned that we wouldn't have enough fuel in reserve."

He pointed out a small refrigerator in front. "Help yourself to drinks and snacks. A meal will be available while we refuel in Denver."

They thanked him, and took their seats for takeoff. They taxied out to the runway, and the pilot revved the motor for a moment, with the brake on. He let off the brake and the plane lurched forward, gathering speed. Marianne took Jims hand as the plane lifted off and reached cruising altitude.

"Need something to steady the nerves," Jim asked.

"I could use a taste," she answered.

Jim went forward and opened the refrigerator. "How about white wine?"

From behind him, Marianne said, "Excellent choice."

"Also the only choice," he said.

Jim found glasses and a corkscrew and opened the wine. He poured a taste for Marianne. She approved so he filled the glass about half way. They toasted each other, then Marianne said, "What are we going to do to fill the time."

"Well, I was thinking we could read a good book, or watch a video."

"Anything else?"

"Well, we could join the mile high club," Jim smiled.

Marianne smiled back.

Chapter Twenty Two
Saturday

After they touched down in Denver, the pilot turned to the co pilot and said, "Why don't you check on our passengers?"

The co pilot went out to the cabin, and came back a moment later. "I think they're sleeping."

"That happens. There's the fuel truck."

In the back of the airplane, Marianne turned to Jim, who was in fact asleep. When the plane landed, she had been jolted awake. She smiled and touched his face before laying down and falling asleep again.

It was just past six in the morning when the plane touched down in Medford. They taxied off the runway. Jim and Marianne collected their luggage and a golf cart took them to the Hertz counter. Jim went in and came out a moment later with a set of keys. They located the car, a Jeep Wrangler, in the lot and loaded their luggage. Jim took the wheel and after finding the freeway, headed north to Grants Pass.

"Honey," said Marianne, "How the hell can you sleep like you do?"

"A trick I learned in the army. I knew the plane would stop midway, so when it did I just went right back to sleep."

"Maybe you can teach me that trick. It would come in handy."

It was just past seven when they reached the small city, then Jim followed the GPS west until he turned off onto a rutted dirt road. Another twenty minutes driving over the road brought them to a command post set up in a converted RV. There were two empty patrol cars and a fire truck parked at the side of the road. Hoses were laid out towards the ruins of an old house.

"This is the place," said Jim.

"Honey, I have a stupid question."

"Go ahead."

"What kind of car did he steal to get out of Hunts Point?"

"It was a Honda Accord, I think."

"Could it have made it up that road?"

Jim thought for a minute. "Good question. We never had to use the four wheel drive, so maybe. See those two cars? The one on the right is a crown Victoria. It sits a little higher than an Accord, but it did make it and it's two wheel drive. He could have."

Marianne shrugged. "OK."

They got out of the car and walked to the command post. He banged on the door, and heard a "Shit" from inside. Then someone stumbled around for a minute and then the door banged open. Jim had his badge in his left hand, held high.

"Seattle Homicide. I was told you'd be expecting us."

The deputy wasn't looking at him. He was staring at Marianne like he'd seen a ghost. After a minute, Jim waved his hand in front of the deputies face. "Can you hear me?" The deputies name tag said, "Lindahl."

"Sorry sir. It's just-hang on a second."

Lindahl reached into the cargo pocket of his pants, then stepped out of the RV. He found what he was looking for and showed it to Jim.

The picture was taken through a window. On the inside of the window Jim could see there had been several photographs. Some of the larger ones had Marianne's image in them.

"Yep, this is the right place. Can you show me where you saw these?"

"Yes sir." They walked through the grass. The area around the house for about thirty feet was scorched. At the back of he house, Lindahl pointed up onto the sagging porch. "Just to the right of the back door. I took that through the window. I was thinking we were going to get a warrant, but Stiina said we had an exigency and opened the door."

"What happened then?"

"Hell happened." Lindahl explained, "he pushed the door open and the place just went up."

"So he had it booby trapped."

"Looks that way. The fire guy said that's what he thought."

"Are they still worried about reignition?"

"What they tell me. Hasn't happened all night though."

Jim took a tentative step up, then another until he was standing on the porch. He carefully shifted to the right.

"Jim, get down from there," implored Marianne.

Just then a board creaked under Jims foot. Jim shuffled back to the left, then stepped down from the porch.

"I could just see through the window. Fire tends to burn a lot of evidence, but there's always something left behind. I can see pictures on the wall in there."

"Ma'am, I have to say you look a lot like the woman I saw in those pictures."

"Deputy, I am the woman in those pictures."

Jim interjected. "Where is everybody?"

"There's three volunteers in the fire rig. Deputy Stiina is in the CP."

"Anyone else?"

"My lieutenant will be here any minute."

Jim walked to the command post. Without knocking he went in and found Stiina half awake in a chair by a computer.

"You're the guy Detective Murray talked to, correct?"

"Deputy Stiina, yes sir. Who are you?"

"Lieutenant Churchill, Seattle homicide. How long have you been out here?"

"It's all starting to run together. I think I've been up for about thirty hours now."

"Put some coffee on."

"Yes sir." Stiina went to a cupboard and pulled out a large tin can of coffee and filters. He got the coffee on and when it was dripping Jim had him put a cup under it and fill it up. Jim poured a cup for himself and Marianne and stepped out of the command post. He looked at Marianne and shook his head. Down the road he could hear a car working it's way up the slope. Deputy Stiina came out. Both Stiina and Lindahl wore wrinkled tan uniforms with dirt stains and were unshaven.

"Do you have tyvex suits and booties in there," Jim asked.

"Some. I can get you a couple sets."

"One for me. You guys can wear one as well."

The car was coming closer. Lindahl went into the RV and came out with three paper suits and three pairs of paper overshoes. The car came past the fire truck and parked next to the Wrangler. A tall trim man got out of the car. He was wearing a clean pressed tan uniform with a white Stetson. A gold bar adorned each collar point. Jim introduced himself and shook his hand. "Thom Housum," he said.

"Thom, can I have a word with you?"

The two men moved off behind the RV. Marianne put on a pair of big sunglasses from her purse and stood silently. The two deputies started putting on the tyvex. After a couple minutes Jim and Thom came back and Thom said to the deputies, "How long have you been here?"

Stiina said, "About thirty hours sir."

"Lindahl?"

"About the same, sir."

Thom spoke into his microphone and issued a set of instructions. He listened a moment then told them, "Someone will be up here in about an hour to relieve you. I want you to assist Lieutenant Churchill as best you can, but do not go into the house."

"Yes sir." The two men started stripping off the paper suits.

"Arson Investigation is probably twenty minutes behind me. They'll do what they can but I don't think anyone is going inside for a while."

Jim went to the back of the Jeep and retrieved a camera from his duffel bag. He told the men to come with him. Marianne stayed behind with Housum.

"You look familiar."

"Really? Have you ever been to Amarillo?"

"No ma'am. Farthest I've been is probably Las Vegas."

"I've been there quite a bit. Maybe you've seen me there."

"So you're a detective?"

"Oh no."

"What are you doing here?" Thom was suddenly wary.

"I'm with him. He's keeping an eye on me."

"Who the hell are you?"

"I'm Marianne Wilson," she said proudly.

"Why is he dragging you here?"

"Oh, we do everything together."

Jim started shooting pictures of the scene from the road. As they walked towards the house he would stop and take another picture every twenty feet or so. He took pictures all the way around the house. When he got back to the front, Lindahl and Stiina took him up onto the front porch.

The front was largely intact. Jim tried the door and found it locked. The windows were covered in soot from the inside. Jim took some pictures through the front window, but they wouldn't be worth much. They moved around to the right. Jim noticed a V pattern on the side of the house.

"I'm no expert, but looks to me like the middle of the house was the seat of the fire."

The two deputies nodded their agreement.

They moved around the outside. Jim shot pictures down the length of the wrap around porch, and through the windows. As he got to the rear of the house, he noticed the back bedroom was pretty much intact. He could see bloody bandages on the floor next to a dirty mattress. As he shot some pictures through the window, Stiina said, "I saw the bandages too. That's why I decided to go in."

"Tell me about that," said Jim.

"It happened pretty fast. The door was unlocked so I pushed it open. Then I heard a pop, saw smoke and we ran like we had a purpose."

Jim shot some pictures through the still open door. "Anything else?"

"I remember it held up for a second. I kept leaning on the door and it broke loose."

"Was that before or after the pop and the smoke?"

"Right before."

"So the door was probably booby trapped. The fire investigators can figure that out."

Jim moved to the window on the right. This room was also intact. The pictures were still on the wall, although it looked like some had curled from the heat. Jim raised his camera and tried to focus on individual photos as well as the overall room. Jim could see pictures from concerts Marianne had played, including the one in Tacoma that he had attended. There were pictures of Marianne in restaurants with a couple different men, having dinner. He recognized one at the Lime that looked like a newspaper photo.

"Did you guys look around for secondary devices?"

"Dammit. Didn't think of it until just now. You see something?"

"Look at the door to this room."

Stiina leaned in. There was a cheap eye screw in the bottom of the door, with a fishing line coming off it. The line led to a small switch attached to a coffee can under the photos.

"Shit. Good eye. They could be trapped in there if it went off."

Jim moved around the porch, taking more pictures. All three of them being careful where they put their feet.

"Tell me what happened when you saw smoke?"

Lindahl spoke. "We had our guns out. Soon as we saw the smoke, we turned and ran off the porch. At first I think we just wanted to get away, then the place went up. We were about there when we hit the dirt." Lindahl pointed to a spot in the grass about thirty feet away.

Jim went off the porch in the direction they had run. "About here?"

"Yeah, I think so," said Stiina.

"What next?"

"We tried to get on the radio," said Stiina," but we couldn't get any reception."

"Cell phone?"

"Neither of us had any bars."

Jim pulled out his phone. He had no bars as well.

"OK. What next?"

"We worked around the house to the cars."

Jim let Stiina and Lindahl show him the path they took through the yard. They had moved in a somewhat circular fashion about fifty feet from the house. The patrol cars hadn't moved since the fire. Stiina explained that he had thought the car might be able to get through with a more powerful transmitter, and he'd been right.

"How long did it take for fire to get here?"

"They're volunteers, mostly. They were here in about a half hour. Maybe less."

"They stay outside," asked Jim.

"No one wanted to be inside. They dumped water on it from out here."

Housum walked over and said, "you bring your girlfriend to all your crime scenes?"

"Turns out she's central to this thing. Look at this."

Jim hit a couple buttons on the back of the camera and the most recent picture showed up. He backed up to the photos of the pictures in the back room.

"That's her," Housum said.

"He's been following her. He's killed at least three people trying to get to her. At least when she's with me I know she's safe."

"She's Marianne Wilson? Doesn't she have her own security? You can't stay with her all the time."

Jim didn't say anything until, "Be sure to tell your CSI and fire guys the house is still booby trapped. You might want your bomb squad. I want to check the barn."

Jim and deputy Stiina made their way to the barn behind the house. Jim continued taking pictures until they got to the door. There were fresh tire tracks coming out of the doorway. Jim walked around the barn to the left. There were four windows evenly spaced on the side. Between the third and fourth window was a small door. Jim tried the door and found it locked. Looking through the window he could see tire tracks on the dirt floor, but the barn was empty.

"What are you thinking," Stiina asked.

"I want to get inside, but I don't want to go in through a traditional door. I think we need to find another entrance."

"You think he booby trapped the barn?"

"I'm not willing to gamble that he didn't."

"Looking at this place, I'm not sure he'd have to."

Jim had to agree. The roof sagged in the middle and the boards were rotting out. When the barn was built, the siding was hung vertically. Jim finally chose a board near the back of the barn, bent and grasped it in his hand and pulled. It resisted at first, then came loose. Jim tossed the board aside, and could now look in. He shined a light around the interior, and could see some boxes and tools laying around, some hanging on the walls. It did not appear that the barn had been used for it's original purpose in a long time.

Jim grabbed the bottom of another board and pulled it loose. Tossing that aside, he did the same with a third board. Now he had an opening he could get through. There was very little light through the dirty windows. Jim scanned the area near his improvised entrance, and stepped through. Carefully working his way along the wall, looking for tripwires and traps. Near the entrance were more boxes and tools. An old water heater lay on it's side, parts of it cut away. Jagged pieces lay close by, some showing signs of having been painted. Jim opened one of the boxes, and saw mostly junk. Looking around Jim saw a pile of trash in the corner, what looked like butcher paper and tape. He opened another box and found three cans of bronze spray paint.

"What you got there?"

Startled, Jim realized he'd forgotten about Stiina.

"I think he painted his car."

"No shit?"

"I think so. Look at this."

Jim held up a piece of butcher paper. Bronze paint traced the edges of it.

"Hard to tell for sure, but I think it's the same color he painted his van. Look over here."

Jim pointed out on the ground where he could see traces of bronze paint in the dirt.

"You're gonna need to update your bulletin."

"I don't think so," said Jim, "I've got other ideas."

They went back out the way they had come in, and walked back to the command post. The arson guy and the counties crime scene investigator were there. Jim briefed them on what they had found and asked that they send copies of their reports to him in Seattle. They promised they would.

Marianne pushed off the wall of the command post and met Jim halfway to the Jeep. He opened the door for her and she climbed in. When Jim got in, she asked what was happening.

"I'm getting you out of here." He told her about the traps in the house, and seeing her picture on the wall of the spare bedroom.

"OK," she said. She was quiet for a moment, then, "God damn it!". Why the hell is he doing this to me?"

Jim was quiet for a moment as he steered past some ruts, then pulled off the road. He picked up the camera and scrolled to the last dozen pictures.

"Who are these guys?"

"Jim…" her voice trailed off, then she got angry. "Christ Jim. These are from months ago. That's Hank, my agent. And that other one is…" She paused for a minute. "Oh shit. That's Brandon Shepherd."

"Who is Brandon Shepherd?"

"After my marriage to Brian broke up, he was the first guy I dated. We went out like twice. Then he decided to go back to his wife."

"OK."

"Dammit. Do not judge me. I did not know he was married."

"Honey, I'm not judging you. I really don't care who you dated before me."

Marianne took a couple deep breaths, then said, "OK." Jim could see she was still angry.

"Do you have his number still?"

"I do." Her tone was clipped.

"When was the last time you talked to him?"

"It's been almost a year. When I told him I knew he was married and that he should go back to her."

"I need the number."

"Jim, I'm telling the truth."

"I know. I still need the number. Honey, he might know something that would help."

Marianne reluctantly opened her phone. Scrolling through the contacts, she gave him the number. Jim punched the number in, noticed that he had just one bar and hit send anyway.

The phone was answered with a gruff hello.

"Jim Churchill here. I'm from Seattle PD. Is this Brandon Shepherd?"

"How do I know that you're a cop?"

Jim gave his badge number, and the number to his office. "Do you want to call them and call me back?"

"Are you from homicide?"

Jim said, "how did you know that?"

"You had a detective come through Memphis about a week ago. What was his name?"

"Jason King."

"OK. I'm, Memphis PD. Billy Holiday. I think we have to talk."

Jim said, "I think we do."

After a few minutes Jim hung up and took in some air. Marianne was watching him intently.

"What did he say?"

There was no sugar coating it. "Six months ago Brandon Shepherd was found dead in a hotel room in Memphis. They've had no leads, but they kept his phone plugged in just in case someone called. Outside of a few people that called before anyone knew he was dead I'm the first one to call that number."

"Oh my God."

"I'm sorry to have to be the one to tell you."

She waved him off. "How did he die?"

"He was stabbed to death in his hotel room."

Marianne sat back in her seat and closed her eyes. Unbidden the tears started coming. Jim wasn't sure what to do. Finally, he touched her shoulder and pulled her close to him. She lay her head on his shoulder and started sobbing. They sat like that for a long time until finally she pushed off him. She reached into her purse and pulled out a tissue to wipe her eyes. Jim sat back and looked out the window. When he looked back Marianne had fixed her makeup.

"What else is there?"

"Not here. Let's find someplace to eat."

"Jim," Marianne stopped, then started again, her tone softer. "I feel like this is all my fault. What is this, five people dead now because of me?"

"Not because of you. You cannot help who you are. He could have helped who he is. He's fried his brain. If it wasn't about you it would have been someone else."

"Let's get the hell out of here," she said.

"You got it."

He had driven all night and stopped in a rest stop near Fife, a ways south of Seattle. He took stock. The wound was healing ok, but he'd have to keep an eye on it. He had food and water and still had some cash. He'd lost some of his gear in the house, but he knew he could sleep in the car. In his bag he found his lock picks. He started working out his plan.

Chapter Twenty Three
Saturday night/Sunday

Jim and Marianne pulled into Grants Pass. They located an Elmers restaurant and pulled into the parking lot. It was close to mid day and neither had eaten since the night before. They went in, and Jim asked for a table in the back. The waitress smiled and said sure and took them back. Jim sat where he could watch the entry. The waitress brought them coffee, then left them alone to peruse the menu.

Jim set his menu down and watched Marianne. When the waitress came over she ordered crepes. Jim ordered scrambled eggs with bacon.

When the waitress went away, Marianne looked at Jim and said, "Thank you."

"What for?"

"Being there."

"I wasn't sure what to do."

"Jim, I don't have, excuse me, did not have feelings for Brandon. Honest, we only dated a couple times until I found out he was married."

"Honey, you don't have to explain."

"I do. It bothers me that all these people are dying because of me. But Brandon was the first one I knew. Why is Bob doing this?"

Jim sipped at his coffee before replying. "Anything I tell you is purely conjecture." Marianne nodded. "I think he believes he is doing right. He was part of your family. I saw how you guys work together, and he was a part of that for a while. Something short circuited in his head, and maybe when you and Brian divorced, or maybe when he saw you with Brandon he knew Brandon was married. Just off the top of my head, I wonder if he has interpreted the Bible and perverted it to his own interpretation. Now he's seeking Gods vengeance or something."

"What happened to Brandon?"

"He came to your Memphis concert. Because he was an up and coming artist himself, he got decent seats. I think Bob spotted him there. After the concert was over, I think he followed Brandon to his hotel."

"Why was he in a hotel? He lived not far from there."

"He was meeting someone. Bob thought it was you."

"No, not ever. Not in a million years. I'd say I was over him, but there really wasn't anything to be over."

"I know."

Marianne looked at Jim questioningly. Then she said in a quiet voice, "Who was it?"

"No one you know. A prostitute named Ellen something."

"What else?"

"She was petite and blond."

"Just a minute," Marianne said, "she looked like me?"

"I think more like resembled."

"Oh god." Marianne was pale.

"You alright honey?" The waitress was hovering, a plate in each hand.

"A little light headed is all," said Marianne. The waitress set the plates down and hurried off.

"Sometimes I forget that you aren't used to this. At work we sometimes have lunch ordered in and talk about our cases."

"Not your fault. I asked," said Marianne.

They finished their late breakfast, paid their bill, then headed back to Medford. They rode in silence for about twenty minutes until Marianne said, "Where the hell is he?"

Jim shrugged. "Wish I knew. We need a plan to flush him out into the open."

They were back at the airport by two. As they were getting on the airplane, Jims phone rang. It was Lloyd.

"I got the call from Billy Holiday. Man that is messed up. How is she doing?"

"About what you'd expect. I don't like sitting around waiting for the next one, do you?"

"No."

"We should be in the office by four thirty. Have Sergeant Worthy schedule a meeting of the task force then."

Jim hung up and they took their seats. Jim pulled out his notebook, and the two of them began going over the file as the plane took off. After about thirty minutes of flying, Housum called. Jim spoke with him for a few minutes then hung up.

"They found meth in tablet form in the house. Also in that same room with the pictures were news clippings. Not just the homicides in Seattle, but Brandon and Ellen."

Marianne nodded.

"Doesn't seem like much. We may never know who his supplier was. It's even possible that he was manufacturing it somewhere. That would explain all of his energy and his psychosis."

They touched down at three thirty at Boeing Field. Marianne used an app on her smart phone to summon an Uber. While they were waiting she went into the bathroom and changed into a white blouse and dark slacks with low heels. When she came out she slipped on a pair of glasses and pulled her hair back just as the Uber drove up. Jim felt a lump in his throat when he saw her.

They loaded into the Uber, and Jim gave the directions to the driver. When they got to headquarters, Jim used his prox card to get in. They drove up to the seventh floor and off loaded the luggage into Jims Explorer. They rode back down to the street level and Jim let him out, again with the prox card. Jim took Marianne's hand and they crossed the street to a coffee shop, where Jim loaded up on a coffee carafe and cups. They crossed back to the headquarters building. It being the weekend, Jim had to use his prox card again to get into the building, then took the elevator up to the sixth floor. They walked into the Homicide office, and saw Lloyd and Ross. Lloyd indicated with his head to the conference room. Jason King and Fred Henderson were at the table. Jason had used the white board to outline what they knew so far. Detective Marlon took a cup of coffee and passed it to MacReady. Sergeant Worthy came in a minute later.

"Where's Daniels," Jim asked.

"He's not coming."

Jim nodded his understanding.

Jim walked to the board and underlined the names Brandon Shepherd and Ellen Duquesne. "These two were killed in Memphis. We did not make the connection to our case until this morning at the Grants Pass fire scene. I could see through the windows that there were a number of pictures stuck to the walls, of Marianne, including one with her agent, and one with Mr. Shepherd." He turned to Lloyd. "Did you get Holliday's file?"

Lloyd held it in the air as he stood. "Brandon was thirty eight. Ellen was twenty two. Brandon was a middle of the road singer and Ellen was a professional woman. Memphis initially thought it might have been a pimp, and also looked at the possibility of a domestic issue as things were pretty rocky with his wife."

Julie raised her hand. "What do you mean a 'professional woman?'"

"I'm trying to be polite. She was a hooker."

Julie lowered her hand. "Thank you."

Marianne had taken in a lot of air, but otherwise looked ok.

Jim looked at her and asked, "are you ready?"

Marianne nodded and stood. "I'm used to having a guitar in front of me. I can't hide for the rest of my career. My job demands that I'm out playing concerts and sometimes smaller gigs. He needs to be found, not just for my sake, but for everyone he's going after because of me. I'm a divorced woman, and after my divorce I dated Brandon twice. Bob worked for me, and knew Brandon but I think he did not approve. He is the one who told me Brandon was married. We played a concert in Memphis, and during the concert Bob disappeared and I haven't seen him since. Bob Lee can fix anything. He'd work on our lights, he could fix the sound system, anything. Our bus broke down once, and he got it running with a Leatherman tool and a roll of duct tape. Also, he's a ghost. We'd need him to move around at the back of the stage and fix things, and he would do it without making a sound. He looks old for his age, but he is wiry and strong."

Jim stepped up. "I want to make one thing clear. He is not a ghost. He is flesh and blood and we will find him."

Julie raised her hand. "I don't understand the connection with Abigail Dunbar. She looks nothing like you."

Marianne nodded. "Sometimes, when I don't want to be recognized, I would wear a disguise to alter my appearance. That appearance somewhat resembles Abigail."

Jim and Sergeant Worthy began assigning tasks. When they were done, Jim took Marianne into his office and shut the door. She started to say something but he stopped her and kissed her once.

"That's the first time you've kissed me since Grants Pass."

"I know. I get caught up sometimes and forget things. I just want you to know I'm proud of you."

She was surprised at his sincerity. She swallowed the lump in her throat and said, "Thank you." They hugged each other tightly.

When he let her go he said, "I need to ask you something."

Marianne braced herself. "Go ahead."

"Brandon?"

"He was an up and coming musician. Probably would have done well. He was polite and friendly and seemed like he might be fun. He asked me out after a show once. We had a good time but I didn't feel a connection. I went out with him a second time, and while we were having dinner Bob shows up. He sits down with us and out of the blue asks Brandon about his wife. I don't think I reacted the way Bob expected me too."

"How was that?"

" I told Bob that Brandon and I were just friends and I knew he was married. He got up and left. I told Brandon that if he wanted anything more than a friendship he would have to resolve things with his wife. And then I got my coat and walked out."

"Bob was stalking you." A statement.

"I think so."

"How did he know you'd be here?"

"I was wondering about that. I had Hank book the room at the Olympus. Do you think he told Bob?"

"I'll put Lloyd on it."

He was backed in, watching the intersection they would have to take. Cars went back and forth, and then night gathered around him. Finally, around seven he saw the Explorer go past, a blond head in the passenger seat. He smiled to himself. "Won't be long now," he thought as he fingered the amulet around his neck.

Chapter Twenty Four
Sunday Night

It was almost midnight. He parked his car in front of the same gate he'd used earlier. The gate was locked, but he had expected that. It only took a moment to open it with the screwdriver. He slipped inside and worked his way from the back yard to the front. He lay in the brush watching the street for a minute. There was no movement. He rose up and darted across the street, sliding to a stop under the bushes in the yard. He looked around again, satisfied that no one had seen him. He took ten minutes to cross from the front to the back yard, where he could look at Churchills house. The porch light was on. He took a pair of cheap gardening gloves from his bag and slid them on.

He took another look around, then in one swift movement stood and sprinted across the street, leaping a hedge by the driveway. He came down awkwardly on his bad leg and winced. He limped across the lawn to the front porch. With his gloved hand he unscrewed the bulb, until it broke contact and went dark. He stepped back off the porch and waited for his eyes to adjust to the dark again.

From the side he looked at the lock. It was a biometric lock with a fingerprint reader. In ten minutes of labor he removed the cover. Risking the light he pulled a small flashlight out of his pocket and played it over the wires. After a moment he used a screwdriver to cross two of the connections and the lock clicked open. The door slid open with a gentle hiss. There was a woman on the other side pointing a rifle at him.

Jim pulled into the garage and hit the button sending the garage door back into the closed position.

"You can take the wig off now," he said to Detective Julie MacReady.

"Thank god. This thing itches," she said as she tossed it into the back seat.

"Hey," said a voice from behind them.

"Come on Jason," Jim said as he got out of the Explorer. Jason handed an AR-15 to Julie and picked up a Remington 870 shotgun. All three were wearing tactical vests.

"Wait here, sir," said Detective Jason King.

"Not on your life. And for God's sake don't shoot the mirror in my bedroom!"

Julie took point as they entered the hall. Jason and Jim checked the laundry room, then they moved down the hall. Julie covered the stairs and the upstairs landing while leaning on the door to the basement. Jim and Jason checked the main floor and circled back, giving a thumbs up to Julie. Jason covered the basement door from the kitchen as Jim and Julie worked their way upstairs. Julie covering the open landing as Jim's Glock led the way up the stairs. A moment later, Jason joined them on the landing.

"I blocked the door with one of your barstools."

Jim nodded.

Jason and Jim checked the master bedroom while Julie covered the hall. Julie led the way into the next bedroom, followed by Jim as Jason covered the hall. Then Jason went into the next bedroom as Jim covered the hall. They worked their way down to the office. Jim led the way in, followed by Jason as Julie found she could cover the basement door. Julie stayed there as Jim and Jason cleared the office then went back downstairs. Julie waited until they were covering the basement, then came downstairs and joined them. The trio awkwardly filed down the stairs into the basement. They worked their way through the gun room, then the music studio and the gym. It was all clear. Jim took the microphone off his vest and said, "the command post is clear." Fred came on the radio and said, "Cameras up, the observation post is clear." The other two teams clicked their mics and checked in.

They went upstairs and Jason went out to the car, coming back with a duffel bag. They set up in the dining room after pulling the curtains. Each of the teams had a set of night vision goggles. The observation post and the command post, which Jim was quietly referring to as the "J" team, had a lap top that was hooked into a network of infrared cameras and sensors. Fred Henderson and Lloyd Murray were in the observation post with Marianne. Francis Marlon and Sergeant Worthy were in the Johnston's house, along with Officer Richards from Seattles canine unit. Ross Nolan and a Medina officer had come in by boat, having been delivered by the Harbor Unit in a Zodiac, they had lowered Jims boat into the water and made coffee in the galley.

"Channel one on the television," said Jim. Julie found the remote and clicked over to channel one. The cameras views were all visible in a pattern on the screen. By clicking on one on the laptop, they could view it in a bigger screen, while the other cameras were still visible on the sides.

"Anyone want coffee? Or a sandwich," Jim asked.

Jason and Julie both chimed, "coffee."

Jim got a pot brewing, then spoke into the mic. "All set here. Stay alert and be careful."

Jason was watching the monitors. Jim brought him a cup and set it on the table next to him, then handed one to Julie.

"How long have you and Francis been dating?"

"Shit, if you can call it that. We've been together for more than a year. But it's tough getting out."

Jim raised an eyebrow.

"We can't go anywhere close for fear of someone recognizing us. Over here on the east side there's a lot of mutual aid. We've helped out a lot of the smaller agencies with some of their major crime issues, so there's a good risk we'll be recognized if we go anywhere. We could go to Seattle but that can be a pain too. So if we want to take in a movie or something we might go to Southcenter or north to Everett. Last summer we went to Chelan. I was in one of the shops while Francis was playing golf and in walks one of our lieutenants. I lied and told him I was with family."

"Maybe not much of a lie if you are living together. Who in your department knows?"

"I'm not sure. I thought we were doing pretty good at keeping it a secret, but Lloyd and Ross figured it out pretty quick."

"Sometimes commanders know without knowing," Jim said, "and we won't say anything unless someone complains."

Julie considered that for a minute, then, "I suppose it's possible Captain Blackwell knows. We've been known to carpool to work, but no one has said anything."

"When Marianne and I started dating," said Jim, "we went to the Lime. The next day her picture was in the newspaper."

"What's that like, being bandied around in the press?"

"Wasn't bad for me. She's used to it I guess. She was wearing a disguise the first time I met her, but she's been wearing it less and less."

"How did you guy's meet?"

"TW Griffin is a friend of mine. I helped organize a business party she was invited to. We just hit it off."

Julie smiled. The kind of smile when she knows someone wasn't telling the whole truth, but decided to let it go. Instead she sipped her coffee and looked at the monitors.

It was just past eleven thirty when Julie called out, "got something!"

Jim said, "bring up camera one." Julie clicked on it, and the image went to the bigger screen. Bob Lee was just shutting the gate behind him.

"He's here. Stay alert," came quietly from the radio.

Jim could sense the anxiety in the air. They zipped up their tactical vests. Jason and Julie slung their long guns on tactical slings and let them hang in front of them.

The three of them watched his progress across the lawns. Jim had to suppress a chuckle when he saw Lee slip and fall, then come up limping.

"He's heading for the front door," said Jason. They watched as Lee stepped onto the porch and unscrewed the light.

They padded into the foyer. Julie kept them back about ten feet. Jason was to her right, shotgun up. Jim was behind them. Jim could feel the Adrenalin kicking in. It seemed to take forever but finally the door hissed open and there he was, face to face.

"Don't move, asshole," said Jim. Bob looked to his right, and saw Marlon, Worthy and a big German Shepherd blocking his path. He looked left and saw Nolan and the Medina officer. In one swift movement he drew his knife and took a step towards Nolan.

Pop! Zzzzt. The Medina officers Taser cracked in the night. Bob screamed and dropped the knife as he fell over backwards into the bushes. One of the Taser probes came loose, and he jumped to his feet, running away from the house towards the street.

"Take him," Richards said, and the Shepherd leapt forward. Bob didn't make it halfway to the street before the dog caught him, grabbing him by the arm and dragging him to the ground. Bob started screaming again. Richards got their first, yelling, "Stop fighting the dog!"

Jim got to him next, grabbing Bob's right arm from under his body and pulling it out straight. He pushed down on Bob's shoulder, pinning it to the ground. The handler called the dog out, and Bob tried to reach inside his hoody with his bloody left hand. Nolan kicked him hard in the ribs, feeling a satisfying crunch. Bob grunted and stopped.

"Police department. You are under arrest," said Ross. He pulled the bloody arm out and handcuffed Bob. Then he reached under the jacket and the front of Bob's waistband. Ross came back out with a rusty .38.

"Shake him down good," said Jim.

Fred and Lloyd and Marianne came walking up the driveway as Ross was searching Bob, while he lay still on the ground.

Lloyd pulled a card from his pocket, and read from it, "Robert Lee, you have the right to remain silent…"

Lee saw Marianne and screamed, "Whore! Adulterer!"

Marianne looked at Lee. "I gave you a job when no one else would. I took care of you. You paid me back by trying to kill me. Go to hell."

Lloyd continued reading Lee his rights. When he was done, Lee looked at Jim and Marianne, and said, "You will both burn in hell."

Jim leaned in. "Maybe. But you'll be the doorman."

Lee sputtered. Someone brought an unmarked van up from down the street. Lee was loaded into it, Ross and Lloyd on either side.

Marianne walked up to Jim and without saying anything, kissed him hard on the mouth.

Julie shifted her rifle to her back, and said, "What the hell," before kissing Francis in the same way.

The Medina officer looked at the two couples and said to no one in particular, "I knew it."

Jim, Marianne, Julie and Francis rode back to the headquarters building in Jims Explorer. Everyone else got into the van after retrieving the cameras. The canine handler and his dog had driven over in an unmarked van.

It was after one in the morning when Jim pulled into the headquarters lot. The van carrying Lloyd, Ross and their prisoner had to swing by the hospital to have the dog bite examined and Lee's ribs x-rayed. While they were waiting, Jason took a statement from Marianne. Everyone else got to their computers to work on their paperwork. When Jason was done with Marianne, she came into Jims office and sat on the couch. Within minutes, she was laying down and sleeping.

Around three Lloyd and Ross came in with Lee handcuffed between them. They walked him to an interview room and handcuffed him to a bolt on the table. Ross waited with him while Lloyd came and knocked on Jims office door.

Jim looked up from his computer. Lloyd took in a sleeping Marianne and a canned energy drink on Jims desk.

"When was the last time you got any sleep?"

"Friday, I think."

"Maybe you ought to take her home and get some sleep yourself. You don't have to watch the interview."

"I got this." Jim drained the last of the can, crushed it and tossed it into the trash by his desk. Then he retrieved another can from his small refrigerator and popped the top. He stuck a note on the door, then closed it behind him after one last look at Marianne.

"How did you know he'd come back tonight," asked Lloyd.

"I wasn't sure if it would be tonight, but I knew he couldn't wait much longer. When we were in Grants Pass, I found an old water heater in the barn. There was a square cut out of it, about six by six inches. The square was in a vise on a bench on the wall. He'd cut a circle out of it. On the flight back I got to thinking about what that could be. Best guess, he was making a full moon. Did you see the amulet around his neck?"

"Yeah, I did."

"Two more weeks to a full moon, but he couldn't wait that long. So he made one."

Lloyd looked doubtful.

"I'm serious Lloyd. He created his own full moon. The guy thinks he's God."

"OK, maybe I can use that," said Lloyd.

Lloyd and Francis went into the interview room and Ross came out. Jim stood behind the one way glass and watched as Lloyd read Miranda to Bob again, this time for the benefit of the cameras. Bob acknowledged his rights, and said he'd talk. Jim thought he looked defeated.

Jim watched as Lloyd took him through the Dunbar murder. He admitted that he'd been after Marianne that night, and made a mistake. Then Francis took over.

"Bob, when was the last time you slept?"

"I dunno. A week ago maybe?"

"How can you go so long without sleep?"

"It's an old trick I picked up years ago. I pop a couple pills, and bam, I'm awake for days."

Francis asked him about Teresa May.

"She slammed on her brakes in front of me. I nearly lost my mind! At first I thought it was Marianne, but she cost me that chance. Then I realized I had to save her too. I went to her house and did what I needed to do."

"So she caused the accident?"

"Damn right she did."

"So you killed her because she caused the accident, not to save her soul?"

"No dammit. She knew she was taking me away from my mission. Her soul was corrupted by Lucifer! I had to free her!" Lee was shouting, his voice raspy.

Francis took him through the rest of it, how he got in, and how he got out. Then Lloyd took over.

"Why did you pick Lisa?"

"I needed to distract you guys. I thought and thought, and then her name came to me in a dream. I looked her up and got the address. She nearly killed me, you know. I want to press charges on her for trying to kill me."

"Let's talk about that. What happened when you went in the room?"

"I was all set to save her. And then her boyfriend attacked me."

"Why did you kill him?"

"It was a total accident. I just swung my arm and he got in my way."

164

"What happened next?"

"She shot me! I was trying to save her and she shot me."

"You were shot in the side?"

"Right here." Bob lifted up his sweatshirt. A bright white bandage, courtesy of Harborview Hospital had replaced the dirty bandage that had been there.

"Bob," Lloyd said, "What happened in Memphis?"

"Memphis is where I got my epiphany."

"What do you mean?"

"At first I thought I could save Marianne by getting rid of her boyfriend."

"Brandon?"

"Right, Brandon. Anyway I went to his hotel. I thought I could talk to him. He opens the door and gets pissy with me. Then he pulled a gun. We fought and I had a knife I used on stage. I stabbed him with it, and that bitch was in there screaming her head off. So I shut her up."

"How did you do that, Bob?"

"I cut her throat. Then I took the gun off the floor and left."

"What happened next?"

Bob took him through going to a pawn shop to look for another knife, and found a set of six knives that he picked up for a song. Then he realized he couldn't go back on the bus. So he stole the van and swapped the plates in Texas. He knew the tour route and almost caught up to the bus in Tacoma, but the van broke down. He'd spent the night in the van until he could buy a part for it, but she was gone. He drove to Seattle and blended in with the homeless population there. He had been downtown when he saw Cassidy Upton get out of a car and walk into the hotel.

"How did you know she'd be in Seattle, Bob?"

"I just had a feeling."

"How did you get the feeling Bob?"

"I just knew."

It was pointless. Lee insisted he had visions, feelings or God spoke to him.

Jim sighed. "Book him. And be careful with him."

"Yes sir," Ross said. It was just after five in the morning. Ross and Lloyd took Bob and walked him back out to the van. They were back before six.

Jim pulled a bottle out of a file cabinet in his office. All six detectives, including the two from Bellevue, and Sergeant Worthy were there with coffee cups. Jim poured a short measure into each of the cups and they

165

toasted the closing of the case. Jim thanked them, then returned to his office. Marianne had not moved. He poured another finger into his cup, and set it on the coffee table next to her. Then he went to his desk and sat down. Reluctantly he reached for his phone and called Alan Dunbar.

"Good morning sir. I just wanted you to know we made an arrest in your wife's case this morning. He's being booked into the King County jail right now. This is a death penalty case, sir. No matter what, he won't be getting out."

Jim listened for a minute and said, "You're welcome sir. I know it's not much, but he won't hurt anyone again." After a moment he hung up.

Marianne hadn't moved, and her eyes were still closed, but she said, "Tough job."

"That part isn't so bad. I just hope he's ok. He sounded really calm."

Marianne opened her eyes and sat up. She took in the coffee cup on the table in front of her. "What's this?"

"After we close a case, all of the detectives involved get a shot. That's yours."

She picked it up, swirled it and tilted her head to pour it down her throat. "Thank you."

"Marianne, I need to know some things."

"This sounds serious."

"I know I can trust you. Do you trust me?"

Marianne thought about it for a minute. "I do."

"How bad are the drugs in your industry?"

"Like anyone else, we have our dopers. Maybe a little more than most because it's young kids with more money than brains."

"Anyone in your band or crew use drugs?"

"There might be a couple. More that smoke weed."

"You ever do anything more than weed?"

"I might smoke a joint once in a while. But that's more for the social aspect."

"I thought you said you trusted me." A statement, not a question.

Marianne sighed. "Someone came out with some cocaine once. I had a fit. He thought it would be funny if he could get me to do a line. Of all people, Bob caught him and told me. He was fired on the spot."

Jim nodded. "Bob said he got started a while ago. But he'd take a pill so he could be up for days."

"That explains some things," she said, "like how he was always up. He was fired from some pretty good gigs, and while no one said so, I had the impression his drug use was getting out of hand."

"Why did you hire him"

"I knew he was a talented techie. He really could fix anything."

Jim nodded.

"What happens now," Marianne asked.

"There will be a probable cause hearing probably tomorrow morning. The judge will likely hold him over without bail. We have seventy two hours to charge. The prosecutor will make that decision probably by tomorrow. Today we have a press conference at two."

"What about you?"

"Well, I suspect I'm in a little trouble with Daniels. He specifically ordered me off the case when I told him about you."

"What does that mean?"

"I suspect I could be reassigned. I hope not, but it depends on how pissed he is."

"Has he said anything?" Marianne was suddenly worried.

"He's avoiding me. He can claim he had no idea I was off the reservation."

"What will you do if you get reassigned?"

"Don't know. Probably retire and write full time. Maybe join a band."

She stood and came around behind his desk and hugged him. "I could make room in my band for you. But I really hope you don't get moved."

Jim kissed her lightly.

She stepped back. "You look exhausted. Let's go home."

"OK."

"I'm driving," said Marianne.

"Honey, it's a department car."

"I don't care. You're dead on your feet. If you don't let me drive, I'm going home in a cab."

Jim handed her the keys.

Chapter Twenty Five

Monday

As soon as they got in the car, Jim leaned his seat back and fell asleep. Marianne had to wake Jim after she pulled into the garage. He staggered upstairs and stripped off what was left of his rumpled suit before collapsing on the bed. He was asleep within minutes. Marianne set his alarm for noon, undressed and climbed into bed next to him.

At noon the alarm went off. Jim sat straight up in bed, clearly disoriented. Marianne was dressed in a white floral print and was brushing her hair out.

"You ok," she asked.

Jim shook his head. "I feel like I could sleep for a week."

He stood slowly and went into the shower. Five minutes later he was out, freshly shaved, looking and feeling better. He dressed in a blue pinstripe suit with a white shirt and matching tie. Jim went downstairs and Marianne followed him. He made coffee for both of them and took a sip. He shivered and said, "I feel human again."

Marianne smiled. "Eat something first," she said.

Jim had forgotten how hungry he was. "Do you want to hit a drive through on the way?"

"Not on your life," she said, "You'll mess up your suit."

Jim looked in his pantry and found a box of granola bars.

"Only three weeks out of date," he joked.

"Hah. You forget I'm a musician. I've had worse."

Jim checked his watch.

"I've got to go."

"I'm not letting you out of my sight today," she said.

Jim knew it was useless to argue. She put her hair back into a ponytail and slipped on a pair of glasses as they went out to the car.

They parked in the garage a little after one. They went straight to Jims office where Jim checked his email. Marianne was on her phone, texting with her band, her manager and Jane when Captain Daniels burst into his office.

"What did you do," Daniels asked. Marianne sat quietly on the sofa, not moving. She wasn't certain that Daniels knew she was there..

Jim looked up from his email, his eyes gone black, and said, "it would help if I knew what you were talking about."

"Robert Lee hung himself in his cell this morning. Lloyd and Ross are up there now."

Jim stood. "Guess I better get up there."

"Forget it. I'll send someone else. Would have been good if you'd told them he was suicidal."

"Captain," Jim said with gritted teeth, "as of this morning there was no indication he would be."

"I'm having a meeting with our chief. The press conference is on hold."

Jim nodded. Daniels left the office, and Jim watched him walk away before he grabbed his coat.

"Jim, he said not to go."

"It's my job. Besides, why do you think he's talking to the chief? He's going to ask that I be moved. He'll probably lodge a complaint for insubordination."

"Well, I said I wasn't going to let you out of my sight," Marianne said, grabbing her purse.

The jail was in the next block. Jim and Marianne walked over and Jim, using his badge, got them both inside and up to the eighth floor. Jim told Marianne to hang back. She stood with a collection of corrections officers as Jim spoke to Lloyd and Ross. They were looking at Robert Lee's body. He'd tied a towel around his neck and tied the other end to the bottom rail of the upper bunk bed. Then he'd used his body weight and just leaned into it, strangling his airway until he passed out and stopped breathing.

"Any doubt it was a suicide?"

"Not really," said Ross. He was the only one in the cell. The only problem is a fifteen minute window the cameras were down in this wing. They noticed him right away when the cameras came back up."

"OK. The ME will tell us what we need to know anyway. Put me down as responding and notified."

"You sure? The captain called and said he didn't want you anywhere near this."

"I know. Put me down anyway."

"Yes sir."

Jim and Marianne left the floor.

On the way back to the office, Marianne asked, "you sure you want to provoke him?"

"I figure he was going to use my non response against me. So I went anyway. He might as well know I was there. After all it is still my damn job."

At three thirty, Daniels came back in, looking upset. He didn't say anything or look in Jims direction, he simply gathered his coat and briefcase and left the office.

Jim raised an eyebrow, but didn't say anything.

The phone on Jims desk rang. Jim recognized the number and said, "guess I'm about to learn my fate."

He picked up the phone and said, "Good afternoon chief."

The assistant chief of investigations said, "hello Jim. Do you have any idea why I'm calling?"

"Frankly, no sir."

"I've been giving this a lot of thought over the last few weeks. I've decided that Captain Daniels needs to move on, you know, for his professional development."

"I'm sure that was a tough decision sir. Who is replacing him?"

170

"I need someone who thinks outside of the box. Someone the detectives will respect. A person who isn't afraid to take a few well considered risks once in a while."

"Who do you have in mind sir?"

"That would be you, Lieutenant." Jim was stunned.

"Are you there, Jim?"

"Yes sir. I'm not a captain, chief."

"I'll see what we can do to fix that. In the meantime you start tomorrow. I'll have a lieutenant in there by next week, so move into Daniels office tomorrow morning. Anything he's got in there box it up and send over to property crimes."

"Yes sir."

The chief hung up. Jim looked at the phone for a moment, before setting it into the cradle.

Marianne asked, "What did he say?"

"You are not going to believe it."

Jim and Marianne were sitting in his dining room, sharing a pot roast with Jane and Sheridan. Marianne told them about the events of the day. Jim was mostly quiet, lost in his own thoughts. When Marianne had finished, Sheridan asked for another beer. Jim shook himself out of his reverie and went to the kitchen. Sheridan followed.

"Jim, what's going on with you," Sheridan asked.

"I don't know what the hell is wrong with me," was the response. "I don't know what I'm going to do when she's on tour. When I go to work, I'm constantly thinking about her. She's always on my mind and the last couple weeks, I was worried about how to protect her."

"Jim, I have to tell you something. You see that woman over there?" Jim looked back to the table where Jane and Marianne were speaking in hushed tones. Sheridan continued, "The first time I met her, I knew I was going to marry her. Even now, she looks at me like Marianne looks at you. Jim, you got it bad, but so does she. Yeah, she's going on tour. And you have more money then sense. I'm sure you can afford plane fare."

Jim thought about it a minute. "I'm such a dumbass."

"Yes you are. But when it comes to love, it turns us all into dumbasses."

They returned to the table. When Marianne looked up, Jim smiled.

"You got a minute?"

"Only the rest of my life."

"Funny you should say that," said Jim.

171

It was dinner time in Knoxville Tennessee. Alan Dunbar was eating alone at Connors Steak house. The pre paid cell phone in his pocket rang. Alan fished it out and answered. The voice on the other end said simply, "It's done."

"How?"

"Suicide."

"Thank you."

He paid for his meal and walked out. He took the battery out of the phone and dropped it into a trash can. The body he dropped in another can. He found his car and drove home.

ABOUT THE AUTHOR

Mr. Dietrich is a long time law enforcement officer in a major police department in Washington State. This is his first book.

www.ingramcontent.com/pod-product-compliance
Lightning Source LLC
Chambersburg PA
CBHW022157240626
47153CB00007B/2712